Praise

"Oh, Jesus! The redem┊   ⋯⋯ moment must have been so overwhelming we could never put words to his experience with Jesus, or imagine the feelings of joy in his soul—the promise of Paradise! *A Man Called Jesus* brilliantly puts this experience into words and captures our hearts."

— Anna L. Hebb, EdD, LCSW, C-SSWS, team editor and co-author of *A View From The Bridge*, inspirations and writings of faith, and founder of Woman of Worth Mentoring Ministries, Inc.

"I have known *about* the man called Jesus since I was old enough to pronounce His name. I have *personally* known Him for the last twenty-five years. The man called Jesus changed my life in some incredible ways. As I read this story, I saw a lot of myself before I came to know Jesus: likeable; the apple of my parents' eyes; loved by my family; deceitful; wanting more than I had; lying to myself and others about my life; fearful, but also having a need, or craving, for something I couldn't, or wouldn't, satisfy. I have since learned that I was not unlike all who do not know this man called Jesus.

In *The Man Called Jesus*, my good friend Tom weaves a realistic and engaging tale about the experiences of a young man caught in a life-threatening dilemma. There comes a time in his life, as it does in ours, that he must make a life-changing decision. As you read the story, apply it to your own life. Know that there are those who love you, think more of you than you think of yourself, who want the best for you, and who will love you unconditionally with forgiveness that most will not believe until it is personally witnessed.

I have been privileged to have a number of people in my life such as Hanan's friend Matthias. Tom is one of them. From their example, I have grown in my life and hopefully have been able to be a Matthias to others. There is a Matthias in your life, too. Open your eyes and your heart and he/she will be there.

Enjoy this story. As you read, and reflect, you will come to see, just as I, Tom, Hanan, Matthias, and so many others have, that it really is ultimately about *the man called Jesus*."

— Bill Vickers

May 2, 2013

Dear Reader,

Thirty-five years ago, I preached my very first sermon. I remember it like it was yesterday. I preached on the repentant thief on a cross from Luke 23:42. Jesus' immortal words, *"Truly I say to you, today you will be with me in paradise"* are some of the most inspiring words ever written in the history of mankind. This simple statement from the lips of Jesus gloriously captures the grace & mercy found only in our Lord & Savior Jesus Christ.

My dear friend and brother in Christ, Tom Lloyd, has beautifully captured the essence of this wonderful moment in the life of our Savior by crafting a historical novella entitled, *"The Man Called Jesus."* In the biblical record, we don't know much at all about this remorseful thief who was saved by Jesus in the last moments of his earthly life. What was his name? What was his background? Where and why did he go wrong? We simply don't know. Tom Lloyd has dared to ask, *"What if?"* What if we knew his name, and knew more about who he was and what his family was like? What if we knew?

A few years ago, Tom's daughter was powerfully moved by the story of this thief who found redemption at the end of his life. She approached her father and asked him to write a story about this mysterious criminal. You hold in your hands the result of a godly man's devotion to his Savior & an adoring father's love for his daughter.

Tom Lloyd takes us on a journey back in time to the days leading up to the triumphant moment when the eternal God/Man Jesus Christ bore the sins of the world and absorbed the wrath of a Holy God in our place. Tom beautifully crafts a story that enhances the biblical record. His work never diminishes the actual scriptural account.

If this story touches your life the way it has mine, you'll walk away from these pages with a heightened sense of gratitude for all that God has done for us in Christ Jesus! The amazing grace of God and the tender mercies of our Savior will become more cherished in your mind and heart.

Thanks to Tom Lloyd and his inspiring story, the repentant thief now has a name...Hanan. You'll march up the hill toward Golgotha with the Roman Centurion named Markus. And the glories of Calvary will be forever etched deeper into your heart & mind.

I am so grateful for this story from the pen of a devoted follower of Jesus Christ, a loving husband & father, and a dear brother in Christ. Well done, Tom!

Mark Jordan

Senior Pastor
Ironbridge Baptist Church

THE MAN CALLED JESUS

THE MAN CALLED JESUS

by T. F. Lloyd

BELLE ISLE BOOKS

www.belleislebooks.com

ISBN: 978-1-9399304-4-6

Library of Congress Control Number: 2015936991

Published by

BELLE ISLE BOOKS
www.belleislebooks.com

There are so many people that warrant the dedication of this book, but they are too numerous to try and list. I will just say it is dedicated to all the people God sent to cross my path who helped me to have a closer walk with Christ.

My family deserves much attention, as my children, grandchildren, and great-grandchildren have all fortified the joy of my salvation as they honor me with their lives and their love.

Reserved for special attention is my helpmate of fifty-seven years. My wife, Louise, is truly the spiritual glue of our family. She has loved me through so much, and I am eternally grateful God blessed me with such a godly woman to walk beside me on our journey with the Lord.

CHAPTER ONE

It was just another morning for Hanan as he awoke to the sounds of his mother kneading the meal and the goat milk into dough. The meal she was using was from one of his nights at work. Even the goat was theirs due to his endeavors.

He could also hear the sounds of carts rolling in the streets, as people rushed to set up their places in the market in hopes of selling their wares. The night before was still a blur and he was physically exhausted from the activities of his work. As he lay on his bed, he thought of the goodness of his father. His father, Nathan, had been a good man, well respected by all who knew him. He had worked hard to supply the needs of the family. Hanan never would be able to forget that day when he was only twelve years of age. He was working in the fields with his father, enjoying tilling the soil alongside him.

Suddenly there was the sound of horses galloping towards them. They turned, surrounded by Roman soldiers staring down at them from their horses. Their swords were glistening, reflecting the sun into his and his father's eyes. One of the soldiers barked, "We have come to take all of your cattle! They are needed for the governor's big feast. Stand aside! We will be herding the cattle across the field."

What happened next seemed to happen so quickly. Hanan heard his father cry out, "No! You cannot take my livelihood!" One of the soldiers drew his sword and cut Nathan down. Hanan remembered how he ran towards the Roman men crying, and then he felt the horse knock him down, the hooves stomping his leg. When he was able to sit up he saw the soldiers riding away laughing among themselves. When he looked at his father lying on the ground, he saw the bloodstained soil they had just tilled. Weeping, he crawled towards his father. When he got to him, he realized he was dead—the man who taught the ways of the Lord and prayed each and every day for his family. Hanan had looked up into the sky and cried, "Why Lord? Why?"

Hanan wiped the memory from his mind and got to his feet, but before he walked into the small eating area to greet his mother, Eunice, he had to wipe tears from his eyes. He walked with the slight limp that had been inflicted on him that day in the field with his father.

"Good morning, Mother, the aroma of your cooking filled my nostrils and woke me up."

"Oh good morning, Hanan," Eunice answered. "I did not hear you come in last night. You must have had to work late." She looked at her son and thought of how hard it had been for him to become the man of the house at such a young age. She was so proud of how he had taken Nathan's place as a provider.

"I tried to be quiet, Mother. I did not want to awaken you."

Hanan's mother was so proud of him for working for their needs. She was always asking him where he worked and how he was able to provide for her so well. It was always a different answer Hanan gave to her. Finally, Hanan said to his mother, "I work for whoever has the place for me." She wondered why he always had to work at night. "What kind of work do you do at night, Hanan?"

Hanan answered, "Mother, there are many people traveling, and they need a shepherd to watch over their sheep and someone to water and feed their cattle." Hanan's answers seem to satisfy his mother's curiosity and he was glad, for he did not want her to know how he really obtained all the provisions he brought home.

Hanan looked around at their humble dwelling place and wished he had learned a trade of some kind, but he was aware most of his neighbors were just as bad off due to the destruction by the Romans. He went over to his mother and said, "Mother, I am not a skilled worker, but my father did teach me how to tend sheep and cattle, and I am able to do jobs that others don't want to do. I clean the stables and work in the fields."

Hanan thought, *I also do other jobs that Mother must not ever know about.*

Whenever Hanan thought about that day his father was killed, his resolve was reinforced to show no mercy to the Romans. He made a point to take advantage of the Romans whenever he observed they were vulnerable. He realized at times he risked his life carrying out his deeds, but he was determined to care for his mother. He felt in his heart the Romans owed his mother and him for taking their possessions and killing his father.

"I'll see you later, Mother," Hanan said as he started to leave.

"Oh Hanan, you haven't even eaten your food yet, and you need to rest before you go to work tonight."

"I'm fine, Mother. I'll be back in time to rest before I go to work, and enjoy the fine bread you are preparing."

Hanan was going to celebrate at a friend's wedding. He stepped onto the street and was met with the scent of a town coming to life. The smell of fresh bread and smoked fish were quite different from the smells of the previous evening's work. Hanan passed by the house where he had been the night before, and even above the noise of the busy people, you could hear the commotion of the Roman soldiers.

Everyone was in a festive mood when Hanan arrived, with

much pleasant chatter among the celebrants. Soon Hanan began to sense the mood shifting, and he began to hear grumbling instead of laughter.

"They've run out of wine," said Hanan's friend, Stephen. "Jesus has told the host to fill the wine vessels with water. I don't think that's going to fool anybody!"

Hanan and Stephen watched as the host instructed the servants to fill the urns with water.

The host dipped some of the water and served his guests. To their surprise, they were sipping not water, but wine—very good wine. One of the men said, "Most people serve the best wine first; you have saved the best for last!"

This man called Jesus had been just another guest at the wedding, but now He was drawing all the other guests closer to Himself as they stood amazed at what they had witnessed.

Hanan felt like he was dreaming and couldn't believe what the man had done. The mood of everyone changed from bickering to celebration.

Hanan observed the gentleness of Jesus, but as he looked at His hands he saw the hands of a working man. *What kind of work does he do? Where is he from?* All of these thoughts entered Hanan's mind as he watched Jesus escape the crowd. Hanan didn't see Jesus again at the wedding celebration. Hanan thought each person at the wedding had been affected emotionally by Jesus, and he realized they all were asking themselves, *Who is this miracle worker?*

Water turned to wine! Who is this man called Jesus? Hanan pondered.

After he got home, Hanan saw that his mother had laid out some bread and baked fish. He ate and tried to get some sleep, but he could not get his mind off of what had happened that day at the wedding.

He tossed and turned until it was dark outside, anticipating the work ahead of him.

Hanan arose and went to find his mother. She was sitting in her favorite place. It was where she so often prayed out loud, and her prayers gave him comfort but also distress as he realized what he was doing to take care of her. His mother was not praying at the moment, but was rather weaving a basket from some vines on the floor.

"Mother, where did you get the vines to make your basket?"

His mother answered, "Hanan, our neighbors are generous to us with their love and sometimes food. Rachel brought them to me to make a basket for myself, but it will be her basket when I finish."

Rachel and Amos lived a mile away, but they still came to visit his mother regularly. They always brought something they wanted to share.

Hanan hugged his mother and said, "I'm off to work now, Mother. I'll see you in the morning."

"I will be praying for you, my son, for our Lord to watch over you. Please be careful."

Moonlight always made Hanan's job more difficult. And the night before him had an exceedingly bright moon. Walking through the town, he heard the Roman soldiers talking and they shattered the quietness of the evening. They were gambling and drinking wine. Hanan could see what he wanted to confiscate, but it would be difficult and very dangerous as well. Hanan's breathing was rapid and he felt his hands shake as he cast his eyes on the golden goblet glistening in the moonlight. It was on a stool beside one of the soldiers who was sleeping. The other two soldiers had left their fellow soldier to sleep it off.

Seizing the treasure would require Hanan to crawl slowly towards the soldier asleep on a pile of straw. As he moved his way toward the soldier, he could feel his heart race, and although there was a chill in the night, he was sweating profusely. The route Hanan was taking had the soldier's back turned toward him. Just a few more feet and he would have his hand on the goblet.

Low to the ground and stretching out his hand, Hanan touched the goblet with his fingertips. He eased it off the edge of the stool, and was about to start his way back, when the guard turned over in his sleep. He was now staring at the closed eyelids of the man only inches away. If the big man awoke, Hanan knew he would be killed. He pulled his arm away and grabbed the goblet, which still had wine left in it, some of which ran down Hanan's hand. Although Hanan was trying desperately to be quiet, it seemed like every move got louder.

It seemed like eternity, but in a short while Hanan was traveling towards the home of Shiam.

CHAPTER TWO

Shiam's establishment was located in a part of town that many people avoided. The streets on the way were filled with drunken Romans and women enticing the soldiers. They were all celebrating loudly. Shiam's door was heavy, but Hanan pushed it open and saw the small man standing behind a wooden table filled with items that were not of much value. The fact that business hours started after dark in Shiam's shop was not lost on Hanan or anyone else. As the light from the single lamp in the corner shone on Shiam, he appeared mysterious and sinister. He was not a person of many words and asked Hanan directly, "What do you have for me?"

As the one who could sell the items, Shiam always got much more for Hanan's goods than he gave to Hanan. But Hanan knew that he himself risked being caught in thievery, while Shiam risked being caught in the marketplace.

Shiam looked at the goblet and asked, "Where did you get this, Hanan?"

Hanan did not like telling Shiam how he obtained any of the items he brought to him, but he said, "I relieved a drunken soldier of his wine cup."

Shiam said, "I will have to melt this down and make it into something the Romans will not recognize. The goblet is worth ten denarii to me."

Hanan answered, "Make it twelve."

Shiam showed his impatience as he said, "You melt it down!"

Hanan was surprised he was offered ten denarii, but the bargaining game between him and Shiam was played each time they did business.

Hanan was tired and did not want to go home so early and wake his mother, so he asked, "Can I stay here the rest of the night?"

Shiam hesitated but said, "You can stay but you have to be out before it is light."

Hanan awoke with Shiam kicking him on his foot. "Hanan, it is time for you to leave!"

Hanan cracked the door and looked down the dark street; all was quiet as he slipped into the shadows of the night. The sun was just starting to show the ugly part of town where he had slept. Hanan saw a few vendors putting their goods out for crowds that would be arriving after sunrise. He purchased some oil, bread and fish along with some flour.

The walk home was filled with thoughts of what had happened during the night, and how he would explain the bounty he had clutched in his hands. He thought of risking his life to supply food for his mother. As he limped through the streets towards home, the limp reminded him of the day it had happened. He thought, *My father was an honorable man that worked in the fields and prayed for God to bless his hard work. I have become the opposite of my father, and surely God is not going to bless my activities. The end will soon be upon me but I hope I can care for Mother until it does.* Hanan shook his head to clear his mind.

He hoped his mother would still be asleep so he could slip in and put the food on the table. He eased the door open and the silence he was hoping for was broken.

Eunice greeted her son. "Good morning, Hanan. I have been praying for you and waiting for you to come home. You must have had to work hard for such nice things for us. Go and rest and I will fix us a meal."

Hanan was emotionally drained and sharing stolen food with his mother caused him to feel the agony of deception.

"I am not really that hungry, Mother. You fix yourself a great meal and I will eat whatever's left later. It is a beautiful day, so I think I'll go for a walk."

Hanan did not know how long he had walked, but he came upon a group of people listening to a man speak. As he got closer, Hanan recognized the man from the wedding celebration. It was Jesus, the one who had turned the water into wine.

Hiding behind a bush, Hanan listened to what Jesus was saying. He kept hearing the word "blessed."

"Blessed are the poor in spirit; blessed all those who mourn; blessed are the meek; blessed are those who hunger and thirst for righteousness; blessed are the merciful; blessed are the pure in heart; blessed are the peacemakers."

Blessed? Hanan wondered how people could feel blessed living such lowly lives. He thought the ones blessed were the Romans, for they had any and everything they wanted in life. Hanan's thoughts went to his mother. *How could she be blessed by my risking my life stealing? What kind of blessing is that? Why were so many people following this man?*

Hanan recalled another man that had crowds of people following him. John, John the Baptist—yes, that was his name. Why had the people followed John? Hanan remembered that the man dressed in animal skins and seemed a little peculiar. Nevertheless, people were drawn to him.

Hanan made his way back home and he saw that his mother had left a plate of food out for him. He realized he was very hungry and devoured the food. In a short while he lay down on his bed to sleep, but he kept hearing the voice of the man called Jesus. He awoke in a sweat, feeling very afraid. Jesus was becoming more and more a part of his life. It caused him to fear.

The words of Jesus were ringing in his head. They sounded familiar, but so distant from his current life. His father had told him stories about God and how God's people survived many trials and tribulations. He never listened intently but, somewhere in the back of his mind, the stories were coming to life because of what he had heard Jesus say that day. He was nauseous as he began to connect his father's stories and the words of Jesus. He walked outside to get some fresh air and clear the thoughts from his head. He thought, *This is the life that has been dealt me by others and I too must survive.*

Hanan had not heard his mother in the house and decided to find her and ask about the stories of long ago. Eunice busied herself each day looking in on neighbors. They had become a major part of their survival as they helped one another.

Hanan found his mother a few minutes later, and he was startled by what he saw. His mother was serving the food he had worked dangerously for during the night. He rushed over and tried to whisper in his mother's ear, but before he said anything, Eunice smiled and said, "Oh Hanan, the Lord has blessed us so much. I am so happy we can help others less fortunate."

There's that word again, "blessed," Hanan thought.

The word stirred his anger even further until he saw the face of his mother. For the first time in a long time Hanan saw what the word blessed meant. He recognized that his mother felt blessed by helping others.

Hanan thought, I will have to work or steal more now that we are feeding the neighbors.

Hanan snapped back to reality when he heard the Roman soldiers passing nearby and talking about the string of thefts.

Hanan said, "Mother, I'm going to rest a while before I have to leave for work."

He felt a knot forming in his stomach, like a tug of war between the benevolence of his mother and his own knowledge of what sharing with the neighbors would mean for him.

With nightfall approaching, Hanan began to think of where he could seek treasures during the night. One of the rules Hanan had followed was not to steal from the same place twice, hoping to confuse the owners into thinking they may have simply misplaced the stolen item. His strategy made Hanan feel he could escape accusations or suspicions.

In the darkness, Hanan limped towards town to begin his search.

CHAPTER THREE

Nightfall provided another opportunity to pilfer from the Roman rulers. It was a dark night with a thick cloud cover, and that provided Hanan good cover for his dangerous activities.

Far into the night, Hanan had not found any opportunities to obtain anything of value from the Romans. He realized his mother had a fair amount of provisions, but now he wanted to do something big that would give her abundance for herself and to share with Rachel and Amos and the other neighbors. He also wanted to be able to cease his dangerous activities, at least for a while. He wanted to spend more time with his mother and also find out more about Jesus. He was about to give up and go home empty handed when he came upon a building that showed a wealthy shadow, even in the night.

Hanan focused on the courtyard and the structure and realized it was part of the Roman government's splendor. His heart raced at the thought of trying to gain entry and then escape unnoticed. He believed inside the walls he would accomplish what he had been thinking about throughout the night. Hanan sat with his back against the wall to rest and think about his strategy for getting inside the walls. His mind was invaded with other thoughts as he closed his eyes and escaped his surroundings. He thought of the day he was in the field working with his father. He remembered the heat of the sun as it shone down on his back while they tilled the soil. It had been a beautiful day until they were surrounded by Roman soldiers, their swords glistening in the sunlight, then commanding his father to give them all of his cattle. He remembered his father resisting, getting cut down by a sword. Hanan remembered seeing his father's blood pooled on the ground they had been tilling. He also remembered how he ran towards the man who had killed his father, screaming uncontrollably, and how the soldier ran over him with his horse. He recalled in minute detail the underbelly of the horse, the pungent odor of the horse's body, and the pain as the hooves stomped him. Hanan not only had a crippled leg because of what had happened, but he had bad dreams, reliving the wild-eyed horse coming towards him.

How long have I been sleeping? Hanan's heart was racing as he realized how he could have been caught sitting against the wall of the Roman courtyard.

The dwelling Hanan spied was where one of the governor's aides lived, and he thought there would be much there that would make tonight a good one for him. This would be the highest Hanan had reached into the Roman chain of command to remove something of value.

If I can gain entrance to this building, I can have time to sit with Mother and hear her tell me the biblical stories like my father used to. And I can spend more time seeking out Jesus, the miracle worker.

The emotions of every job of thievery had always begun the same way: fear and excitement wrapped up in an exhilaration that drove him forward. This one felt different though. Maybe it was because this was not taking from the Roman soldiers, but the home of a Roman official. His eyes and ears were his tools for not getting caught, as they saw and heard every detail of what was in front of him as he moved along the wall.

The ground was sandy and when Hanan would take a step he could hear the crunch of the sand. He removed his sandals and placed them by a fig tree close to the stone wall that surrounded the courtyard. The sand cut into his feet, but his bare feet did not make a noise as he eased his way closer to the house. There were four guards within the courtyard, and they each held a position where they could view the areas near the house. Hanan decided his only chance of getting within the walls of this dwelling was to wait and watch—wait and watch for the guards to perhaps get sleepy and not realize what was happening in the night.

Hanan was about to give up and return home when he heard the voices of the guards. They evidently decided no one would dare attempt to enter the courtyard and face instant death. They were on the far side of the courtyard, and they were gambling. Hanan knew that if their superior or the master of the house caught them they would pay a big price for leaving their posts. Hanan wondered why they would take the chance of being caught, and then he saw why. There was a fifth guard walking the perimeter. He was watching for things, and of course would warn them if anyone in the house stirred.

Now Hanan thought, *How do I get past this one guard?*

He got his chance when the patrolling guard stopped to talk with the other four men. Hanan's heart was beating heavy and although the night had a chilly air, he was far from being cold. He crawled along the wall, searching for the best way to gain entrance to the courtyard.

CHAPTER FOUR

Hanan saw a gate that did not have a lock on it, but a sliding bar that he would have to slide without making a noise. The bolt squeaked as it was moved. Hanan spit on the bolt again and again until it moved without making a sound. He knew he would have to close the gate, open it, and close it again before he could escape after his take for the night. Once inside the courtyard, Hanan crawled toward the house. All the while he was watching the guards gather in the corner of the courtyard. He knew he had no cover as he crawled across the ground. If the guard looked his way, he would be killed by the Roman soldiers, just as his father had been slain. He thought the guards might hear his heartbeat as his chest pounded on the stone courtyard, and he hoped if anyone was inside the house that they were all asleep. Hanan started to crawl back to the gate and leave, but he was now up against the wall of the house and he would be undercover here as long as the guards did not return to their stations.

The door Hanan pushed against was secured from the inside, so Hanan eased his way to one of the windows on the side of the building. The first window was open. There was an oil lamp burning and there were pallets on the floor, but no one was lying down on them. There was a doorway that led to another room. Hanan could see that he would have to make it to the back wall of the house. He hoped there would be a window there where he could look inside. Rounding the corner of the house, he saw another window. As he slowly he made his way towards the window, he suddenly heard a voice outside the wall. He looked and saw another Roman soldier coming through the gate.

Hanan knew he had spent most of the night wandering about and sleeping, and he could see the sky was losing its darkness, which would expose him. His heart raced and he was wet from sweating, which made the sand stick to his skin.

Hanan heard the soldiers laughing. The new soldier said, "So you play while the master's away?"

"We guard an empty house, and it is good to have him away for a few days," said one of the guards. This was music to Hanan's ears. He now knew no one was inside the house.

With that news, Hanan eased himself through the window. There was an oil lamp burning on a table, and it provided light for Hanan to see what was in the room, but he realized it would also make him visible to anyone looking in. So he crawled along the floor and into the larger room. Hanan sat with his back against the wall. He was exhausted, and in this position he could survey the room.

His eyes gazed upon something reflecting from the light of the lamp. Hanan crawled towards the glowing object. He raised his hand to touch the object on the table. He ran his fingers along what seemed to be a chain of some sort. Slowly he gathered it up and held it up for the dim light to reveal what was in his hands. It was a heavy gold chain, and it had some type of stones embedded along its surface. It must be a necklace that would be worn by the one who was away. It would be too heavy to wear on a journey. It must be for special occasions, perhaps when he was with the governor.

Now to get it out without being seen.

Hanan decided the best way to carry the jewelry was to put it around his neck under his cloak. He began his long trip to the court gate by crawling his way along the floor and out of the window. The gold chain around his neck made it more difficult to crawl along the stone courtyard. Hanan wondered where the guards were. He could not hear any voices or sense any movement, and fear gripped his heart as he slid against the wall. He waited a long while before he began to move slowly towards the gate. Hanan suddenly heard the soldiers and realized they were standing outside the wall beside the gate.

What can I do now? thought Hanan.

He froze and for the second time that night, fear gripped him so tight his muscles ached and he could not move. He was thankful he had not moved out of the shadows, so he was safe for the moment. He saw the gate, his exit, but knew he could not move in that direction. He knew that though the sun had not begun to show the orange and yellow rays of first light, it had to be close. He looked towards the back of the house and thought it would be a better place to be than where he was. This seemed to relax his muscles. He worked his way to the rear of the house and tried to gather his thoughts. A sense of being a caged animal was growing in his mind, and he felt his legs and whole body shudder at the thought of being captured.

For the first time since his father had been killed, Hanan began to pray. *God deliver me from the Romans and I will never steal again.*

CHAPTER FIVE

Leaning against the house, near the window where he had entered to steal the necklace, Hanan was desperately looking for another exit.

A chilling breeze blew in Hanan's face, and he looked up to see a branch of a tree swaying in the wind, and it hung over the wall. With a good jump he could catch hold of the limb, but he felt the weight of the gold chain around his neck, and wondered if he could jump high enough to catch hold of the limb. His first jump reminded him of how heavy the necklace was, and the ache he still had in every muscle. The branch was looking to be out of reach.

After several tries, Hanan caught hold of the limb and made it to the trunk of the tree. Sliding down the tree, he felt a sharp pain and almost cried out, but he held his breath as the pain increased. He felt along the trunk of the tree. He had sliced his chest on a sharp pruned limb. He was bleeding and could feel the blood running down his body. He looked up the tree as his feet touched the ground, and saw a piece of his cloak that was torn away when he raked his body over the sharp limb. The chain around his neck had broken apart and was now hanging loosely down from each of his shoulders.

Hanan was able to crawl out from the wall and made his way across the sand. The sand burned into the cut on his chest and he wanted to scream, but he held his tongue. Hanan looked over to where he had left his sandals and knew he had to leave them, for the guards would see him if he tried to retrieve them. Hanan was troubled. He had left a piece of his clothing in the tree along with his blood. He also had left his sandals. Was his loot worth it all? Later in the day he would take the gold chain piece to Shiam and see what he could get for the jewelry he had risked his life for.

Hanan felt wetness on his body. It was a mixture of sweat and his bloody chest. He did not want his mother to see his clothes or his wound, so he went to the river and stripped off his clothes. He wrung his clothes out several times, and laid them on the bank, as he washed his wounded chest. The water was refreshing, but his chest had a deep wound and it stung when the water splashed across it.

Hanan looked up out of the water and saw a Roman soldier staring down at him.

"Now what might you be doing this time of night? This is not a public bath water for the likes of you. Now get going!" Hanan took his cloak that was already torn and made a bandage for his chest. He then pulled the wet robe over his head and began the painful journey home.

CHAPTER SIX

Hanan hid the jeweled gold piece under his bed. He had made it in the house without awakening his mother and he found some dry clothes and lay across his bed. Exhausted, he went into a deep sleep. *"Blessed are the poor in spirit, blessed are those who mourn, blessed . . . "*

"Hanan! What happened to you?" His mother's voice awakened Hanan with a jolt. "Oh Hanan, what happened to your chest? Let me look at it." Hanan raised his body off his bed and felt the sharp pain across his body. "Mother, I'm fine. One of the cows gored me while I was attending them. I'm fine." Hanan did let his mother change the bandage on his chest, and he drank some goat milk along with eating some bread and fish his mother had fixed for him.

"That's the last of the flour. But don't you worry about it. I know the Lord will provide for us."

Each move was painful as Hanan moved towards the door, so painful he changed his mind and laid back down. He drifted off to sleep thinking about what Shiam might think of the treasure he would bring.

The wind brought Hanan awake as the aroma of different foods being prepared for the evening meal filled his nostrils. He especially delighted in the sweet aroma of bread being baked.

"Mother, I'm going to town to get my money for last night's work. I will be back soon."

Eunice answered, "Please come home and rest, Hanan. You need to let me care for you."

"I will, Mother. Don't worry, I will be fine."

Hanan had traveled the road into Jerusalem so many times he felt he knew where every bump and crevice was, and he always enjoyed the smell of the cedar trees as the sun drew out their special fragrance. Hanan walked slowly, for his chest hurt, but he wanted to see what Shiam would give him for the treasure he was carrying under his cloak.

The road to Shiam's humble shop had a few more Romans walking the streets than usual. Hanan approached the door to the shop and entered.

"Hanan, what happened to you? You walk like an old man." Shiam expressed concern as he asked, "What do you have for me this time, Hanan? I don't see you carrying anything."

Hanan started to reach up and remove the gold necklace from around his neck, but it caused so much pain he groaned and grimaced. Shiam got a glimpse of the gold piece when Hanan's cloak was rolled back.

"Stand still, Hanan, let me get what you have under your cloak."

Shiam pulled the heavy gold chain from around Hanan's neck. "You have outdone yourself this time, my friend."

Hanan asked Shiam how much he would give him for the jeweled piece.

"Hanan, this golden chain with the jewels is worth a lot. But it must be sold as it is to get the price. It will take me time to move it. I'll give you forty pieces of silver in advance and will give you much more after I find a buyer. I will have to travel away from here to move it. Hanan, this will be missed by the owner and a handsome reward will be given to the one who tells who stole it. I am in this trickery with you, so you do not have to worry about me saying anything, but you must lay low for a while. It will also draw many questions in the market place. It would be best if we didn't see each other for a while, and if you become a good citizen while this settles. Give me a few days, and if you need more money, come to me."

Hanan stayed in the long shadows as he made his way to the market. He saw lots of people surrounding the fish vendor, and he moved towards them to pick up some smoked fish.

A loud booming voice called out his name, and Hanan almost buckled at the knees. Hanan turned and saw Simon the fisherman. "How are you, Hanan?"

"I am well, Simon. I know now why there are so many people here today. The catch must have been good."

Simon laughed and said, "Hanan, I no longer fish in the traditional way. I have been following the new Messiah. He asked that I become a fisher of men." Simon continued, "How is Eunice doing, Hanan?"

"She is doing well in spite of father's unmerciful death at the hands of the Romans."

"Your father Nathan was a great man, Hanan, and a good friend. I wish he could have been here to meet Jesus. He would surely have been a follower, and would want you to be one as well. Hanan, have you heard the good news?"

Hanan felt the shame rush over him as he considered the question. His father had taught him about the scriptures, and he remembered hearing him talk about the promised Messiah. Hanan knew Simon was going to tell him that Jesus was this promised one.

"No, I haven't," Hanan answered, "but I have been watching the healer from afar and wondering."

"Healer, yes, but He is much more, Hanan. He offers us a

chance for healing in our soul—a healing your father so much wanted for himself. His bitterness for the Romans proved his undoing."

"So it was my father's fault they killed him?" Hanan screamed.

Simon began to laugh. "Hanan, you sound like your father. He just wouldn't let things move on until they were right. Jesus offers us this opportunity by healing the soul of the bitterness we carry. Hanan, I see you carry the same weight of the past your father did. This weight can be lifted."

Hanan was quiet. He knew something was real about what Simon was saying. He had felt it. But the anger of the Romans was still so strong and fresh in his heart.

Simon saw that Hanan's thoughts were drifting away and said, "Hanan, tomorrow at the fountain come and meet Him. See for yourself the healing He offers."

With that Simon left Hanan at the fish cart. Hanan bought some smoked fish for the week and other food before heading towards home. The pain in his chest and the growing pain in his head were more than he could handle. He wished he had his father to talk to.

CHAPTER SEVEN

Hanan decided to take Shiam's advice and not go out at night for a while. Since he did not want to lie around and get weak, he decided to seek out the man called Jesus.

Sleeping at night was new for Hanan. He lay in bed and considered the many things that had happened in the past two days. He had received his largest sum for the gold chain with the promise of more. He had nearly gotten caught at the river. Now he had Simon on his mind. Simon's words were whirling around in his head like a storm on the ocean.

He was reminded when he turned over of the large gash in his chest. The pain was less than the night he had received it, but he could still tell it was there when he moved.

He awoke for the first time in a very long time with the sunlight coming into their humble home. Eunice was busy preparing the morning meal as Hanan walked into the open cooking area.

"Good morning, Mother."

"Hanan, I didn't hear you come in this morning."

"I did not have to work last night, Mother. The man I do most of the work for will be out of town for a few days. He said he would contact me when he returns."

Hanan's mother was happy he would be home for a while and that she would be able to care for his injury. She also gave thanks to the Lord for their food.

Speaking with a mouth full of smoked fish, Hanan asked his

mother, "Mother, why was Father so bitter at the Romans?"

Eunice paused and stared off into space before she spoke. "Your father had watched so many in the community lose all they had by decree or tax. He carried their sorrows in his heart and worked hard to make sure they did not go without. The extra work and fear of when they would come for his property was a huge burden to carry. The day the Romans came, I can only imagine all the anger and bitterness that came out. The bitterness cost him his life. I loved your father, but he was a proud and honorable man who did not care for the wrongdoings of the Romans.

"Hanan, I see some of the same struggles in your eyes that your father had. I pray each day that God will take these burdens from you."

"Oh Mother, I can handle myself," said Hanan.

Eunice bowed her head and walked away. She had heard that before.

Hanan pushed away from the table. "I'm going for a walk."

"You should rest until your wound heals."

"I will be fine, Mother. We can look at the bandages when I return." He needed to clear his head, and a walk would help him sort out all the demands being placed on his mind.

Hanan walked through the countryside with no direction. When he woke from his reverie, he was looking at the fountain where Simon had said to meet him.

Hanan saw Jesus talking with one who was crippled. Hanan moved closer to the pool and heard the crippled man say, "No one will lower me into the pool." Jesus spoke and the man rose to his feet, walking and leaping.

Who is this Healer? Hanan had seen this crippled man in the market begging on many mornings!

Hanan began moving towards Jesus, working his way through

many who were sick or dying. Hanan paused for a moment while an old man was being moved towards the Healer, then looked up—his knees buckled and his heart raced and he felt as though the whole world stopped, because his eyes met the Healer's eyes! Mesmerized by the contact, Hanan felt unclean to be so close. He couldn't explain any of his feelings; he just knew he had to get back.

The crowd began to move and follow Jesus. Hanan kept his distance but watched the men who seemed to be attending to the miracle Healer.

There were twelve men who were always with Jesus. Hanan knew them as disciples of Jesus. He was told Jesus had chosen them to walk with Him. Hanan saw Simon and Andrew, who made their living fishing. He saw two other brothers, James and John, the sons of Zebedee, who also made their living by fishing. He knew them and wondered why they gave up all they were doing to follow Jesus.

Simon, the fisherman, moved in Hanan's direction away from the other disciples. Hanan waded through the crowd and greeted him. "Simon, it's me, Hanan."

Simon greeted Hanan with a brisk slap on the back, and Hanan could barely hold back the pain that rushed through his chest. Simon was a big man with a full, rich black beard, but when he opened his mouth, his big smile was usually followed with a big belly laugh. Today was no exception as Simon smiled and declared, "Hanan, you decided to take me up on my invitation!"

"Who is this Healer?" Hanan asked.

Simon's eyes seemed to get larger as he replied, "Hanan, Jesus is our Messiah and He has come to deliver us from our sins."

"Where is He from?"

Simon said, "He is from Nazareth. Come, let me take you to meet Jesus!"

Hanan let Simon lead him forward a few steps, but then he stopped and told Simon, "Simon, I cannot go with you today, but perhaps another time. I need to go and check on my mother now."

Simon hugged Hanan and said, "Give my greetings to your mother Eunice. Both of you must come and meet Jesus, God's Son. You will be blessed when you listen to His teachings."

Hanan thought of his life and wondered if this teacher would consider him worthy of His blessing.

CHAPTER EIGHT

Each day, Hanan witnessed supernatural events at the hands of Jesus. One day the huge crowd following Jesus had become hungry. There was a young boy in the crowd with a basket that held five loaves of bread and two fish. The offering of food was small, but Hanan watched Jesus bless the limited amount of food, and it miraculously fed everyone there, with some left over.

Hanan's troubled mind wondered, *Is this God sent to earth?* He thought for a moment he could run down from the grassy knoll where he was standing and find the peace he desired, but a confession would destroy not only his life but also his mother's heart.

During the time Hanan had followed Jesus, he had seen him feed the large crowd with just a few loaves of bread and fish and heal people. Hanan mingled with the crowd as he tried to find out more about who this Jesus really was.

Each night, Hanan went home. It was good to spend time with his mother. It was also good to follow Jesus each day.

CHAPTER NINE

Finishing dinner, Hanan and Eunice walked out to three tossed and worn chairs that Nathan had made and sat in the shade of an old sycamore. The empty chair was always there because neither of them wanted to change the arrangement.

They lived about a mile from Jerusalem. Their neighborhood was surrounded with a rocky terrain where wildflowers managed to grow in patches between the stones.

"Mother, do you remember the times Father and I would go to the valley and pick the wild grapes?"

Eunice smiled. "Those were the good days. I would do my basket weaving while you played in the trees. Sometimes I thought you would break every limb on those trees."

"Why did God let father die?" asked Hanan.

Eunice was searching in the sky for an answer that had eluded her for so many years. "Hanan, God has a plan for all of us, and it is ours to hear His plan and be obedient. Sometimes we don't listen very well. I try hard to listen to what God would have me do in my obedience. I do things but don't understand why, but just know it is what He wants. Your father struggled with listening even when he knew. Simon tried hard to help your father understand that the Romans were a part of God's plan for him."

Simon has invited me to meet the man he now follows, Jesus. Simon claims He is the Messiah. "Mother, what are you hearing from your friends about Jesus? He is performing so many miracles."

"Hanan, some of my friends are among the crowds following Jesus, and I don't know what to make of it all. The prophets proclaimed a Messiah would appear and would release the captives, but I do not know if it is this man or not."

"Simon is one of Jesus's twelve chosen disciples. He told me he was now a 'fisher of men.' I have been near Jesus when He has healed the sick and caused the lame to walk. He is no ordinary man."

Hanan's mother reached out and touched his hand. "Hanan, what a blessing this is for us if Jesus is truly the Messiah we have longed for and prayed for. I would like to pray right now while we are together. Hanan, please pray with me."

Eunice squeezed Hanan's hand as he bowed his head. She began to pray. "Lord of our fathers and maker of heaven and earth, we have suffered at the hands of men, but You have blessed us by giving us our daily needs. Help us not to be bitter or have anger in our hearts but instead cause us to remember all You have led our people through and to believe You will lead us to dwell together where Nathan dwells. We want to believe the man called Jesus is the promised One. Open our eyes and our hearts as we seek to proclaim Him our Savior sent from heaven."

Eunice opened her eyes. "Hanan, this man is the Messiah. He has been foretold by many. Go to Simon, hear the Messiah!"

Hanan felt a gentle breeze blow across his face, wet from the tears streaming down, and his nostrils were filled with the pleasant aroma of the wildflowers his mother held. But most of all he felt a warm and comforting spirit within his heart. He went to his mother and as he hugged and kissed her he said, "Mother, your obedience is so comforting to hear. I want the peace that you have in your heart, and to be able one day to forgive the ones who killed my father and your husband."

It seemed like just a short period of time had passed since he and his mother began their special time together under the sycamore tree, but as he looked up into the sky, Hanan could see the sun setting in the midst of clouds streaked with shades of purple and red as daylight was ending.

Hanan and his mother shared a meal together that evening. As she was cleaning up, Hanan said, "Mother, I enjoy hearing your prayers and we will seek out together to see if Jesus is our Deliverer. I want the peace that you have in your heart, and to be able one day to forgive the ones who killed my father and your husband, Nathan."

He rose to leave the room. "I have really enjoyed our time together today. I love you."

"I love you, son, and our time together is very special. I forgot to tell you about our friend Lazarus. Rachel and Amos were by today, and they say he is very ill. I will be praying for Lazarus as I end my day, and would like for you to have prayerful concern for him as well."

"Good night, Mother. I hope you rest well. I will have Lazarus in my thoughts, too."

CHAPTER TEN

Several days had passed since Hanan and his mother had talked about Jesus. He was feeling much better and physically all that bothered him from the night he hurt himself on the tree was a long jagged scar across his chest.

He continued to follow Jesus from afar and hoped to one day have nerve enough to actually speak to Him. Each time the thought entered his mind, he felt unworthy to approach the man of miracles. Hanan also realized that if Jesus was really sent by God, he wanted his mother to meet Him face to face, too.

It had become easy to locate Jesus, simply by looking for the crowd of people that followed Him. When Hanan caught up with the crowd on this day, he heard people saying that Lazarus had died. Lazarus was well liked by everyone, devout in worshiping the Lord. He was a small man physically, but commanded respect by the way he lived his life and loved his close-knit family. He worked the land, and it brought forth food for his family. His sisters Mary and Martha loved their brother and enjoyed pampering him. Hanan knew they would grieve and miss Lazarus greatly.

Hanan remembered how his mother, Eunice, had prayed for Lazarus to return to health. He followed the crowd as Jesus led them towards Lazarus's home.

When they arrived, the air was filled with weeping and despair. Mary and Martha cried out to Jesus and told Him that if He had been there, their brother would not have died.

Could this man have prevented the death of Lazarus? Hanan thought perhaps He could have, for he had watched Him heal a crippled man.

Hanan was told that Lazarus had been dead for three days and buried in a tomb. Jesus told them to open the tomb. Hanan thought the smell of death would turn the crowd away as well as himself.

With a commanding voice, Jesus said, "Lazarus, come forth!"

Some among the crowd started to murmur and snicker, expressing their disbelief with those around them, but they did not receive any support for their ridicule, for there were many that truly believed that the man they had witnessed heal the sick and cause blind eyes to see would reunite Mary and Martha with their loved one, Lazarus. The crowd grew silent, except for the few who were snickering at the very thought this man Jesus could raise the dead.

Everyone stared in amazement when they saw Lazarus, with burial clothing still attached, walk out of the tomb. This Jesus had just raised a man from the grave! Hanan wanted to go closer and be like the twelve men with Jesus, but he was filled with fear at the thought of his own life as a thief. He thought Jesus could take his life as quickly as he had raised Lazarus. *Jesus goes about doing good,* Hanan thought, *but I go about doing evil.*

Hanan realized the news of Lazarus's death would bring sadness to his mother so he wanted to hurry home and be the bearer of the good news that Lazarus was well and of Jesus's miraculous power. He hurried home and found his mother sewing a patch on the cloak he tore on the night he stole the gold necklace.

"Mother, I have some exciting news for you. Remember how you prayed concerning Lazarus?"

"Yes, Hanan, I have been praying for Lazarus, and also for Mary and Martha. I know they are so concerned about their brother."

"Mother, I have witnessed a miracle that has stirred the people following Jesus. It is hard to believe, but I saw it with my own eyes."

"Hanan, sit down and rest. You are shaking and your eyes are showing that you have been frightened. Please sit with me and I will pray for God to give you peace in your heart."

Hanan sat down in the chair next to his mother and said, "Mother, three days ago Lazarus died."

As Hanan paused, his mother began to weep. "Oh Hanan, we must go and try to help Mary and Martha as they mourn the loss of Lazarus."

Hanan took a deep breath and said, "Mother, the miracle that happened concerns Jesus. It is true Lazarus died three days ago and was placed in a tomb, but this man called Jesus raised him from his grave! I was there, Mother. I watched as Lazarus came out of the tomb. Mother, I know you have been praying about Jesus and wondering if He is sent by God. After what I have witnessed, I do believe Jesus is no ordinary man. He must be the One John the Baptist has been preaching about. I will do everything I can to have you meet Jesus. I want you to be touched by Jesus and receive His blessings."

Eunice's hands were trembling as she lifted them up and said, "Oh God, it is true. You have sent us our Savior! Praise Your name for delivering us once again from bondage. I pray that Hanan and I may be touched and blessed by Jesus."

Hanan did want to experience the blessing he had seen others receive from the hands of Jesus but his thoughts were telling him he did not deserve to receive such a blessing. He thought of Lazarus and his mind was penetrated with the thought, *You are not a Lazarus.*

CHAPTER ELEVEN

The next morning Amos and Rachel came by to see Eunice. Rachel's voice was filled with excitement as she said, "Eunice, we are going to see Mary and Martha and share in the glorious event in their life! We want you to go with us and hear how the man called Jesus raised Lazarus from his grave."

Hanan heard the voices of Amos and Rachel and came into the small sitting room to see them.

Before Hanan could greet their guests, his mother said, "Hanan, I am going to go with Amos and Rachel to visit Mary and Martha, and I am sure Amos and Rachel would not mind if you go with us. I want to hear the good news from all at Lazarus's home."

Hanan was excited about the possibility of hearing any more news about Jesus, but he already had plans to see Shiam to get more money.

"Mother I have to go into town today, but I am so happy you are going and I look forward to hearing about your visit."

Hanan hugged his mother goodbye and headed towards Shiam's house.

He was glad to see Shiam was home and anxious to find out about the gold necklace. Shiam seemed to be very upset and ill at ease.

"What is wrong, Shiam?" Hanan asked.

"Hanan, haven't you heard? The chain necklace you stole was a most valuable piece of jewelry. The guards were put to death and there is a search going on to find the one who stole it. It seems they have a piece of torn cloth that was left hanging on a tree, and they say there were blood stains on the tree. They also found a pair of sandals. Hanan, you just don't know the trouble you have brought me. The gold chain necklace you stole is worn only on special ceremonial days. The governor has ordered that his aide be put to death if it is not found. The piece belongs to the governor, who issued it out to his aide for a special ceremony that was to take place. Hanan, I cannot dispose of this troubling piece of jewelry. I have lived in fear they will come and search for it, and I know they would put me to death. I cannot give you any more money for it. In fact, I am going to give you the piece back."

After telling Hanan he could keep the money he had advanced to him, he said, "Hanan, don't bring me anything else. You should have been satisfied to take small things. You're too dangerous for me to do business with."

Shiam went into a back room and returned with a folded blanket. Hanan knew what was within its folds. It was the heavy gold piece.

"The blanket is yours to keep, Hanan. Take it and what is wrapped inside of it and leave. I never want to see you again."

He abruptly pushed Hanan outside and shut the door. Hanan stood there for several minutes before he started towards home. He knew if he was found with the gold piece that he would be killed. Hanan realized they would search to find the jewel piece and that there would be a reward to find the thief. He knew he could not take the gold chain home. The Romans would kill his mother along with him if they found it there.

He found himself standing by the river and he sat down on the bank to think about what to do. *Blessed are those who mourn. Blessed are the poor in spirit. Blessed are the meek. Lazarus, come forth!*

Hanan awoke and found himself trembling and cold in the darkness that had settled around him. What had happened? *Did I dream or was it real?* Hanan unfolded the blanket and let the heavy gold chain fall to the ground. He wound the blanket around himself, and reached down and picked up the shiny gold jewel and tossed it into the river. He cursed it as it disappeared under the water. Hanan's thoughts now were about how was he going to care for his mother. He realized Shiam was right. He should have stayed with the small items that were easy to bring money for him and his mother.

Hanan was about to leave the bank of the river, when suddenly a hand grabbed his shoulder. Hanan looked into the eyes of the Roman soldier.

"What are you doing here? I've run you away before. Speak up or I will toss you into the river for the fish."

Stammering, Hanan tried to tell the soldier a story that would be believable. "I've come to the river to seek fish for food."

"What kind of fish? What would you catch fish with? You have no net. I saw you toss something into the river. What was it you threw into the water?"

Hanan stammered even more, but a story came to his mind and he blurted it out. "I had a net, a big one, but it was too large for me to handle and it slipped from my hands when I cast it into the water."

Would he believe the story? Hanan wondered.

"Be gone, you poor excuse for a fisherman."

The soldier laughed and mocked Hanan as he gathered up his blanket and limped towards home. He was going home empty-handed, knowing his mother needed oil and flour.

Lightning flashed across the sky and the wind began to blow harder than Hanan had ever felt. He wrapped the blanket around his face, as the wind was blowing sand that stung his skin. As the lightning flashed, he caught a glimpse of a boat on the water, dipping down into the waves. It looked as if it would surely capsize. Hanan looked as the lightning flashed again, and he saw a group of men in the boat, but one of the men was standing up, looking out over the water. The man he was watching had his hand held up with his face into the wind. Astonishingly, the water became calm, with not a ripple across the surface, and the wind became but a gentle breeze that felt soothing to Hanan's face.

What had happened?

Hanan walked slowly along the riverbank in hopes he could see the boat with the men in it. He paused a moment and listened to the noise in the night. He heard water splashing, and as he stood there, he knew what the splashing water was. It was the sound of oars rowing a boat. He walked farther up the riverbank, and then he saw the empty boat on the shore. He also saw the twelve men there, listening to Jesus as He drew them close to his side. Hanan wanted to run down to the beach and beg Jesus to let him be a part of that group, but he thought of the shame in his life. He felt unworthy to receive the blessing of the Holy Man.

He recognized the voice of Simon as it penetrated the stillness that was now present. All of the voices rang with excitement as they gathered around their holy leader.

CHAPTER TWELVE

When Hanan made it home, he was exhausted, hungry and afraid. He could not sleep as he thought of his mother in need of food, how he was nearly caught by the guard, and how close he was to being put to death. He lay with his eyes open with thoughts of his peril, but he also thought about Jesus. Hanan realized he must try to find out more about Jesus, about who He was and how He performed such miracles. As he drifted off to sleep, Hanan thought, *Tomorrow, maybe tomorrow.*

Hanan awoke to the smell of food. He thought surely he could smell the aroma of warm bread, and he found his mother standing by the table, upon which sat bread and a bowl of fruit.

"Come, my son, sit down eat and let me tell you about how God visited me during the night."

Hanan listened as his mother spoke with such excitement in her voice. He wanted to interrupt her and tell her about how Jesus calmed the storm with the raising of His hand, but his mother had more to tell.

"Hanan, the strong wind blew our door open and after the storm was gone, I went to close the door and on the step was a basket of food. I don't know who brought it to us, but what a blessing has been given to us this day."

Hanan's head was reeling from the restless night, but as he witnessed his mother's tears of joy he felt an emotion he had never felt before. Who gave us food? Who traveled through the storm to help us?

"Come, Hanan; let us give thanks to God for supplying our needs. Hanan, sit with me and enjoy this wonderful food."

Hanan bowed his head as his mother prayed. He heard her words and wished he could believe as strongly as his mother that God would care for them. Hanan's thoughts caused him to fear not being able to care for his mother, but perhaps even more so the Romans finding out about his taking the golden necklace.

Would Shiam tell the Romans the whole story? Surely he would fear punishment from the rulers for the part he had in the crime. His thoughts were interrupted by the sound of his mother's voice.

"Hanan, you seem to be troubled by something. What is it that you are so concerned about? You do not have to worry about providing for me. Look at the food God has given us, and rejoice with me for His goodness."

"I'm sorry, Mother. I am thankful for all we have, it's just that so much has happened over the past days, and I am trying to understand it all."

Hanan started to tell his mother about what he witnessed during the storm, but instead he shared his mother's excitement of feeling her prayers were being answered.

"You know, Hanan, ever since the holy man Jesus has walked among the people, so much good has happened. Before I go to be with Nathan, I want to meet Jesus."

"You will, Mother. I promise that I will help you meet Jesus. I want you to be touched by His holy power. It is amazing to see all the miraculous things He has done for the people. I was just thinking of how wonderful it would be to have Jesus here to talk with you. I know He would enjoy your company as well as your cooking. We will find Him soon, Mother."

"Oh Hanan, don't you worry. God will let us know when and where to meet this blessed one. I will pray and wait for our Lord's timing."

"Mother, I have enjoyed being with you this morning. It is so good to see you happy and enjoying each day."

"I am happy, Hanan, and the time we have together is a precious blessing for me."

The pleasant thoughts Hanan was enjoying were interrupted as he thought about the gold necklace and caring for his mother. He thought, *Jesus could be the answer for Mother. She is so close to God and Jesus has healed people, caused the wind to be still, and even raised a man from the grave. I must find a way to get Mother to be touched by Jesus.*

It was a beautiful day for a walk, and the meal had given him new strength. As he approached the city, Hanan could hear voices of a crowd. He saw a woman who was trying to get through the people. Looking down the hill, he could see her pushing and pulling through the crowd so she could be close to Jesus.

Hanan found Jesus with the same twelve men. Hanan joined the crowd and looked over at the woman who was trying to get closer to Jesus. The woman was knocked to the ground and the crowd ignored her as she crawled through the feet of Jesus's followers. Hanan was intrigued by this woman's desperate endeavor to reach Jesus. Hanan came closer to the woman, pushing through the crowd to see her.

He was also closer to Jesus and he felt his heart beating rapidly. Hanan saw the woman's hand reach forward to grab the hem of Jesus's garment. Her hand barely touched the hem of His garment as He passed by. Hanan felt sorry for the woman and he worked his way even closer toward her, but he heard a voice say, "Who touched me?"

Hanan thought it was odd for anyone to ask that question because everyone was touching someone as they sought to get closer to Jesus.

Hanan thought of his mother and how she wanted to meet Jesus, but he didn't want her to have to crawl through a crowd of people on her knees to meet Him. Hanan could feel the emotion of the woman as the people ignored her, and he was drawn to also crawl through the rushing of feet to just touch Jesus. This was the closest he had been to this holy man, and his heart beat rapidly within his chest.

Hanan was almost in touching distance of the woman and he was about to help her up when Jesus turned around and said, "Thy faith hath made thee whole."

Hanan saw the woman rise to her feet, a new strength in her demeanor and tears streaming down her face. He felt himself rooted to the ground, astonished by the scene that had just unfolded before him. Though he willed himself to follow Jesus and His disciples as they began walking down the road, his attention was focused on the woman. He could not see her anymore, but he could hear her laughing and talking loudly with people as she worked her way back through the crowd.

Hanan looked down the road to see if he could still see Jesus, but He was gone. Hanan wanted to talk with the woman, but she too was gone. He saw some of the people the woman had been talking with and went up to them.

"Excuse me," he asked one of the men, "do you know that woman?"

"Oh yes, she is well known around here. She's been sick and feeble for twelve years."

"What about doctors?" Hanan asked. "Have they tried to help her?"

"None of the doctors have been able to help her, but today she says Jesus healed her."

"Have you ever met Jesus?"

"No," the man replied, "but I have seen with my own eyes the healing of this woman."

"Do you know any of the men Jesus calls His disciples?"

The man leaned forward and with a gleam in his eyes answered, "I know some of them and this man called Jesus must have been very persuasive to get them to give up everything and follow Him."

"Have you not heard about the miraculous things Jesus has done?" Hanan asked.

The man seemed to be growing impatient as he replied, "Look, I have heard news about healings and even that He raised someone from the grave. I have also heard He was from Nazareth, and I can't help but wonder what good could come from there."

CHAPTER THIRTEEN

Hanan started towards home, thinking of Jesus as he walked. He wished he had crawled with the woman on the ground and touched Jesus's garment with her. He could approach Jesus that way, he thought, but he could not walk up to Him and address Him directly. Hanan also thought it was probably his last chance to get to know who this healer and peacemaker was.

When Hanan arrived at home, he found his mother sobbing and her body shaking. Her head was pressed against the table as she moaned. He ran to his mother and hugging her he asked, "Mother, what has happened? Why are you crying?"

He felt tears of anger form in his eyes as he looked around and he saw most of what they owned scattered around on the floor.

Hanan's voice quivered as he asked, "Who did this to you, Mother?"

With a weary voice from crying his mother said, "Please sit down, Hanan, and hold my hands to keep them from trembling."

There was a long pause. She took a deep breath, then said, "Hanan, while you were away two Roman soldiers pushed open the door and shoved me to the floor. They asked me so many questions. They asked if I lived alone and I told them I lived with my son. They wanted to know where you were and I told them you had left this morning and were probably in town. Oh, Hanan, they plundered the entire house, looking for what I don't know. I have been trying to get things back together, but my shoulder is in pain from hitting the floor so hard. They tore your room apart, and I'm so afraid. Hanan, what could they possibly want from us?"

"Mother, I am so sorry you had this happen to you. What can I do to make you feel better?" Hugging his mother, he said, "I will get things together. Please lie down and rest."

As he straightened the house, he told her that he had heard someone had taken a valuable piece of gold away from the Roman rulers and that they were probably looking for it at everyone's house.

"Oh Hanan, I hope no one has what they are looking for. They would surely be put to death."

Hanan was sorry he had brought so much trouble to his mother and he thought of Jesus and wished He would walk through the doorway.

Once things were in order, Hanan sat on the side of his bed and wept. He remembered the last time he had cried was when his father had died. He also wept thinking about his mother, and about the difficulty he was having in caring for her.

After a sleepless night, Hanan went to his mother's bedside and asked, "Mother, can I get you something to eat? Do you want me to go and get Rachel to stay with you a few days?"

"Oh Hanan, I am very sore from my fall and it would be good if you could stay close by me for a few more days. All I want now is some water to drink."

Hanan brought his mother a cup of water and said, "Mother, I will be here to watch over you. I just have one errand to do. I will not leave you alone long."

It bothered Hanan that he had to go and ask others for food, but he was on his way to do just that as he walked hurriedly towards Amos and Rachel's home.

Amos greeted Hanan. "Hanan, it is good to see you. How are

you and your mother Eunice doing?"

Before Hanan could answer, Rachel entered the room. She asked the same question that Amos had. "Hanan, how are you and Eunice doing these days? Is there anything we can do to help you?"

Hanan hesitated but finally said, "Mother was hurt by two Roman soldiers yesterday. They invaded the house and knocked Mother to the floor. She is feeling poorly. I have come to see if you have any food to spare for her."

Rachel was holding back tears as she said, "Hanan, we do not have abundance but what we have we will share. Sit down and rest while I get you some water to drink, and then I will prepare a basket with the food we have. I am going back with you to stay until Eunice is able to get around on her own."

Hanan's heart was filled with appreciation and he said, "I thank you for your kindness and will repay you as soon as I can."

Amos spoke with a voice of compassion as he said, "Nothing will be owed us for sharing what God has graciously given."

Hanan had to ask: "Did any of the soldiers come to your home, Amos?"

"Yes, Hanan, they came. But after questioning us about whether we had any other family living with us, and seeing we were too old to cause them harm, they walked around looking for something. I believe they were looking for that expensive jewel that was stolen some time ago. I guess they figured we could not have accomplished such a feat and they left. I'm sorry they were so rough with your mother. Maybe we had different soldiers than the ones who came to your home."

Hanan thought, *They found out at our house my mother lived with her son, and thought it was possible he had taken the jewel necklace.*

CHAPTER FOURTEEN

W hen Hanan and Rachel arrived, they found Eunice sitting up in her bed praying. When she had finished her prayer, Rachel said, "Eunice, Hanan told me what the soldiers did to you. I am so sorry you were treated so badly. I have brought some food, and I am going to stay with you a few days."

"Rachel, thank you for your kindness I will fix us something to eat."

"No, Eunice, you rest and I will see that we have a meal. You must let me care for you until you get your strength back."

Hanan could see that his mother was in good hands, and he also realized there was not enough room for all of them in their small living quarters, so he said, "Mother, I am going to work, and I might be away for a few days. I will bring more food when I return."

He thanked Rachel and left to find how he could accomplish the task of getting food for his mother.

Nightfall was upon him as he walked along the dusty road towards Jerusalem. He heard the cooing of a dove penetrate through the olive trees, and as he passed the fields where sheep were herded for the night, he heard their bleats. It was a peaceful solace for his troubled heart.

The only work Hanan knew was what he learned from his father, and that was caring for sheep and cattle and working in the fields. Losing his father as well as all of their livestock had left Hanan without obvious livelihood, leading him to do whatever he had to in order to care for his mother. It crossed Hanan's mind that he could possibly become a beggar, but that caused him to feel as much shame as the stealing.

His mind was in a spin as he thought, *Why didn't I try being a fisherman like Simon? Maybe I could have learned a trade, something besides working in the fields and something other than stealing!*

Hanan walked among the people, his mind on how he could obtain food for his mother. He talked with many people and also listened to the news they had about the Roman rulers. All the people he talked with had been visited by the soldiers, who told them they were looking for something of value that had been stolen. Hanan listened as one man told him the Romans would put to death the man who stole from the Roman rulers.

Hanan asked everyone he met about Jesus. He expected to hear only good news regarding Jesus, but instead, he heard words of anger from some of the men. They told him Jesus was causing trouble for their families.

Hanan met a man that he recognized, named Matthias. Matthias had been a friend of Hanan's father, and he asked Hanan how his mother was doing. Hanan wanted to tell Matthias that all was well, that he was able to care for her, but feeling the friendship of Matthias and the struggles in his heart, Hanan told him how poorly they were doing and that he was in town to seek food for the table.

Hanan was tired and hungry and he poured out his heart. "Matthias, I know you and my father were friends. He often talked of you within our home. Up until now I have been able to care for Mother, but I find myself unable to provide for her as I once did."

"Hanan, I remember the day your father was killed, and I know it has been hard for you since that day. After that happened, I along with others moved my family away from the city. We formed a community in the rough terrain near Nazareth. There we are not bothered by the Romans as the people near the city are.

"Hanan," Matthias said, "God has been gracious to me and my family. God be with you and your mother, and I will be by to visit with you both and will bring food. I want to talk with you and your mother about a man called Jesus. Hanan, have you heard about Jesus and His miracles?"

"I have been following Jesus from afar and have witnessed His miracles, Matthias, but I haven't been close enough to actually meet Him. I want Mother to meet Jesus because she talks about Him a lot."

"Hanan, the people in my community believe Jesus is the Messiah sent by God to free us from our bondage. Many have been healed and blessed because of His miracles."

"Matthias, I know it will be a blessing for my mother to see you again. Thank you for wanting to help us."

Hanan wandered over to a group of people gathered together around an open fire. They were cooking some fish and eating strips of bread they had baked over the fire. Hanan was very hungry and was about to beg for something to eat, when one of the men called to him, "Come here, lad. Join us and give us company."

Hanan sat down with the men, thanking them first before he began to devour the food like a hungry animal. He realized conversation had ceased as he looked up and saw they were staring at him with much concern in their eyes.

"How long since you have eaten, young man? What is your name?"

Hanan wiped his mouth with his arm and said, "Please forgive me for being gluttonous. My name is Hanan." He told the men about his mother and about how his father had died at the hands of Roman soldiers. Hanan continued on, revealing how he had come to town to beg for some food but couldn't find the courage to do so.

Hanan learned from the men that they lived in the mountainous area, a distance from the town. They said they were not bothered much by the Roman soldiers, who thought the area to be barren. The leader of the group of men was a man named Amon. He said, "We are able to grow some of the food we eat, along with fishing and hunting wild game. Perhaps you and your mother would be better served by coming to live in the hills away from the city."

Hanan's mind was racing with so many thoughts from today's activity. First Matthias, now Amon. Hanan answered, "How will I find you and your people if my mother agrees?"

Amon smiled and said, "Head toward the town of Nazareth. The closer you get to Nazareth, you will find people that know me well. They will direct you to me and my people. You can inquire about a man called Matthias and also ask of him. Matthias is well known and respected by the people. You and your mother will be taken care of, I assure you."

Then Amon asked something that gripped Hanan's heart. "Have you met Jesus, the Messiah sent by the Lord?"

Hanan spoke. "No, I have not met Him, but have witnessed His miracles from a distance.

Amon was an old man, and as he struggled to stand up, his eyes were glistening with excitement. "Hanan, I had an encounter with the Roman soldiers somewhat like your father did. They took all my livestock and destroyed our home. I resisted and pulled one of the men from his horse. It was a foolish thing for me to do but he was about to assault my wife. The soldier twisted my leg until he broke it. They all laughed as I crawled on the ground with my wife and children bending over me crying. My heart was filled with so much hate for the Romans, but then one day I listened to John the Baptist preach about Jesus and how Jesus was the Son of God sent to be our Savior. I watched as John baptized Jesus that day, and everything seemed so peaceful. God seemed so near and my heart released the anger it had been harboring for so long. I believe Jesus is the Messiah sent by God. I think maybe one day Jesus will be close enough that my leg might be healed, but if not I still walk with love in my heart instead of hate. Jesus has been sent by God to establish His earthly kingdom."

Whereas Matthias was small in stature, with gentle, light eyes and a white silken beard, Amon had dark eyes that seemed to look into the heart of a man. He also had a dark beard that matched the darkness of his eyes. If Hanan had not experienced the kindness of Amon, he would have judged him to be a hard taskmaster.

There is only one king, Hanan thought, *and it is Caesar.* But he realized something was happening that he could not explain. He wondered if this Jesus would really set up a kingdom and rule them.

Hanan thanked Amon and bid him goodbye. Amon gave him some fish and bread wrapped in a cloth and said, "Take this to your mother and God go with you."

Hanan remembered that Rachel was with his mother and it was late in the night, so he found a place to spend the evening in a stable. He felt comfortable lying down with the sheep and goats for he had spent much of his life with the flocks and herds of animals.

Hanan's mind was spinning when he began his journey home. He thought of all the things Matthias and Amon had said to him the night before. He wondered if he and his mother could move to the community where Matthias lived.

He arrived home and found his mother in bed. He knew something must be wrong for her to be in bed so early in the day. He went to her bedside to check on her, and when he sat down on the bed, his mother stirred. She raised herself up and said, "Oh Hanan, I'm sorry I could not fix you a meal today, but we do not have oil or flour."

Hanan choked on his words as he answered. "Mother, I have food for you. Please get up and eat. Where is Rachel?"

"I sent her home, Hanan. I knew she wanted to go home and be with Amos, and I am feeling much better."

She arose slowly, explaining that the fall she had from the Roman soldiers caused her to be very sore. Hanan had to help her up and to the table, and he unfolded the cloth with the food he had received from Amon. He told his mother how he had obtained it.

"Oh Hanan, God heard my prayers today. I asked Him to supply us food. Hanan, God sent the man you met today."

Hanan told his mother about meeting Matthias, and that he promised to visit them today and that he would bring food. This further confirmed his mother's thanks to the Lord for supplying their needs.

"Hanan, Matthias is a good man. I remember how kind he was to us after Nathan was killed. He moved his family somewhere near Nazareth, and it has been a long time since I have heard from him."

Hanan's mother pushed back from the table, but she wasn't able to stand up by herself. Hanan lifted her to her feet and led her back to her bed, but she said, "Help me to my chair so I can sit and talk with you."

Hanan eased her into her chair and draped a blanket around her legs.

"Mother, have you been hearing anything more about Jesus?"

"No, I haven't heard anything since last we talked. I do know that something is happening, and I believe God is causing it all to take place. I still believe it is the man called Jesus that God has sent to us."

They both heard the knock on the door, and Hanan went to see who was there. It was Matthias with two large baskets of food.

"Hanan, I hope I am not interrupting you, but as I promised I have food for you and Eunice. Is your mother here?"

Hanan led Matthias into his mother's bedroom, where she was almost asleep in her chair.

"Mother, we have a visitor."

Hanan's mother raised her head up and opened her eyes to see Matthias. Matthias smiled and said, "Forgive me for interrupting your nap, but I had promised Hanan a visit today. Eunice, it is so good to see you again. Your husband Nathan was a good man. My name is Matthias; you probably do not remember me."

Hanan's mother tried to get up, but she could not stand. Matthias gently told her not to get up, that he would sit on the floor.

Eunice began to recall some of her memories, and yes, she remembered Matthias and how he worshiped the Lord. "Matthias, it is good that God has brought us together again. I wish I could prepare you a meal, but we have run out of food. I know God will take care of us though."

Matthias said, "Worry not about feeding me, Eunice, for God has been gracious to me and my family, so I have brought you some food. I will see that you have food each day. It brings joy to my heart to share what God has provided. I want to tell you and Hanan the glorious news about a man called Jesus. He was sent by God to deliver us from suffering. He has proven Himself to be who He says He is. He claims to be the Son of God. I believe it to be true. He has performed many miracles and healed the sick and the blind. He has caused the lame to walk. Only God could do all these wondrous things."

Eunice had a smile on her face as she said, "Matthias, will you pray for Hanan and me right now? I feel God's presence here with us and I want to praise Him for all He has done for us."

"I will gladly pray with you and Hanan, Eunice, for I too feel God's Spirit reaching out to us."

Matthias stood up and went to Hanan's mother and placed his hands on her head. He prayed, "All merciful Lord, Creator of all things, I pray that You will bless this house and all who enter. Our hearts are heavy, yet we will rejoice that You have sent one to deliver us from bondage. I pray You will be with and comfort John, the one who baptized even Your Son. Be with him in the Roman jail and give him the comfort of Your spirit. Glory be to you, oh Lord our God."

When Matthias was done praying, Hanan asked, "Why have they arrested John the Baptizer?"

"He was arrested because he disturbs the Romans. They were upset he had a following, and they would not have anyone come between them and the people. I pray he will be set free."

Hanan watched as his mother began to rise up from her chair and he went to help, but astonishingly she stood erect on her own and clasped her hands with Matthias's.

"I know God has sent you to us this day and I pray that this man called Jesus truly is our Savior and Messiah."

Matthias asked for a cup of water and said he wanted to talk to them about another matter. They went into the room where the two baskets of food were sitting on the table. Matthias moved the baskets aside and asked if they would sit and listen to what he had to say.

As they listened, Matthias told them about where he lived. He asked them to consider moving there, where they could be cared for in a better way. "So much is happening near the city and the rulers are closer to their subjects. The soldiers patrol the city and nearby areas regularly but they rarely come to our community. We supply them with fruit and vegetables and they see we pose no threat to their authority."

Matthias continued, "We are not completely ignored by the rulers, but they feel we are away from where we could cause trouble, and are merely a people living and helping each other. We are not in need of morsels of food the rulers would hand out to a begging people. Within the city, people are much of the time feeling the rough hand of the Roman authority. Even the temple leaders can cause the people problems—they are given special treatment by the Romans and will sometimes turn on their own. It is sad to see how many have become beggars as they bow down to the Romans."

"Mother, I think it would be best if we go with Matthias. I want you to be better cared for, and it all seems to be coming together."

Eunice raised her hands in the air and said, "Hanan, we barely have a roof over our heads, and you have worked so hard to provide for our daily needs. You have done well, but I feel God is leading us to follow. Matthias, I am ready to go."

I will be away from constantly looking over my shoulder and wondering if I will be captured for stealing. Hanan thought of being in jail with John the Baptist and wondered what they would do with the prophet.

They packed what few items they could take with them. It was not an easy task, for though they had very little that was of value monetarily, they had numerous items collected through the years. Hanan patiently helped his mother select the things they would be carrying to their new home.

As they went outside, Hanan's mother stopped for a moment and looked back into the house. He knew she was having second thoughts about moving, as he saw tears in her eyes. "Mother, we do not have to go. I will look after you here."

"No, Hanan, I am ready. I just wanted to stop for a moment

and thank God for watching over us here in this house. He will be with us in our new home. It is good. It is a good thing and I know it is according to His will that we leave."

Matthias had a cart pulled by a donkey, and Hanan placed their belongings upon it.

Hanan saw that his mother was holding on to a cloak of some kind, and he asked, "Mother, what do you have? Do you want me to put it in with the rest of our things?"

"No, Hanan, I wanted you to know that I have mended your cloak that got torn that night. I know the material doesn't match very well, but it still will provide you with warmth when it is cool."

Hanan took the cloak from his mother and tried it on, and he glanced down and saw a piece of material the color of purple that his mother had sewed on his red cloak. He hugged his mother and thanked her, and they began their journey.

This can be a new beginning, Hanan thought as they left, taking with them many pleasant memories as well as some sad ones.

CHAPTER FIFTEEN

Shiam was sleeping peacefully but was awakened abruptly by the sound of his door being pushed open. He jumped to his feet but immediately felt rough hands dragging him outside. The soldiers tied his hands and feet and threw him on to a cart. He tried to ask them a question, but the blunt force of the soldier's fist made his jaw ache with pain. Shiam cried out as the soldiers shoved him into a dark cell at the jail. They untied his hands and feet and tossed him onto the floor. They secured the lock on his door and he heard the stomping of their feet as they went away. He wondered why he was in jail. Then he thought about the last stolen item Hanan had brought him. Had Hanan told the rulers that he, Shiam, had stolen it to gain a reward? Shiam realized why he was in such a predicament, and his thoughts wandered back to Hanan and to that cursed piece of jewelry that Hanan had brought to him for money. His pain, fear of what was going to happen to him, and anxiety for his future kept him rolling and tossing through the night.

∞∞∞

Matthias, Eunice, and Hanan had been traveling at the donkey's pace in the cart filled with the meager household goods. It was a rough road and they were bounced around and jostled about. Matthias guided the donkey over to a grove of olive trees as the sun was getting low in the sky and said, "Let us stop here awhile and rest. We have been traveling for some time and the donkey could use a break as well. Hanan, just over that ridge is a stream of water. You can get the donkey some water and replenish our water supply as well."

Hanan had just crossed the top of the hill and was headed towards the creek when he heard hoof beats. He climbed back up the hill to look out towards the road, and he saw two Roman soldiers on their horses. They had stopped alongside the donkey cart and were questioning Matthias. One of the soldiers had dismounted and was searching inside the cart. Hanan heard the soldier ask, "Where are you headed with this cart full of junk?"

Matthias very calmly answered, "We are on our way home and we just stopped to rest. We live among those that bring the fresh fruits and vegetables to the governor and the quarters of his guards."

The guard who had been searching the cart's contents mounted his horse and said, "You had best be on your way. It is getting dark and this road is traveled by thieves."

The soldiers rode off and Hanan realized if he had not been hidden from their view he could possibly have been taken back to Jerusalem. He looked up at a sky with stars beginning to appear and a moon that would light their way for the rest of their journey. He dipped up the water and headed back to his mother and Matthias.

"You missed meeting our company, Hanan," Matthias said. "We had two Romans soldiers visit with us while you were gone for water."

Hanan felt guilty for not telling Matthias he had seen the soldiers as he answered, "I hope they did not cause you any trouble, Matthias."

"Hanan, they were very kind to us and were concerned for our safety as we travel this road at night," his mother replied.

Hanan was glad he was not there to be seen by the soldiers, but he also felt he probably would one day face the Roman rulers for his misdeeds. He realized moving would not be an escape from the eyes of those determined to find the one who would dare to take a treasure from them.

Upon arriving at their new home near Nazareth, Matthias introduced Hanan and his mother to some of the people in the community. Amon recognized them and came to greet them.

"Hanan, my friend, it is so good to see you. How is your mother? I hope she is well."

Hanan introduced him to Eunice. "Amon, both Mother and I are so thankful for what you and Matthias have done for us, and Mother is looking forward to making her home here."

"Good! That's very good, Hanan. Let's go and see the new home that Matthias has made ready for you."

"Oh yes," said Eunice, "let us see what the Lord has prepared for us."

They followed Matthias and Amon to their new dwelling place. It had more space than the home they had left.

Matthias unhitched the donkey and left the cart outside of the door. He held up his hand and said, "Come, Amon, let's let our friends get settled and rest from their journey."

Hanan's mother went about the house touching things, and thanking God for everything.

"Hanan, it is God's will that we be here. Hanan, let us give thanks to the Lord."

She asked Hanan to pray like his father had prayed, but Hanan answered as he always did at her requests for him to pray, "Mother, you are closer to God then I am, and I enjoy hearing you pray."

Hanan thought of all of his narrow escapes while living the

life of a thief. He never asked God for protection, for he felt God would be upset with his stealing. He also felt unworthy to call upon the name of the Lord.

That next morning, many people brought blankets, milk, flour, oil, and bread. Along with all of this, they also enjoyed the cooked fish brought by Amon. The only thing that Hanan had been able to give the community was the goat they brought with them.

As the days passed, Hanan found many things he could do, and he enjoyed working in the fields again, tending the sheep and helping care for the elderly. He was so delighted to see his mother smiling and happy. Hanan said to Amon, "I appreciate all you and the community have done for us."

Amon laughed and said, "Hanan, you and your mother have brought much joy to all of us, and you are a good worker. You are not a stranger here, my friend. You are family."

Hanan walked outside and a fresh breeze blew against his face. Hanan thought, *Will I be able to live here without anyone finding out about my past?*

CHAPTER SIXTEEN

Time had passed, but the determination of finding who stole the governor's jeweled necklace had not diminished. In fact, the failure of the soldiers to find the necklace or the thief had infuriated the governor. If something of this magnitude was left unsolved, he reasoned, the rulers would appear weak and vulnerable. The guards were growing anxious about what kind of reprimand they would face if they didn't solve this crime soon.

Several of the elite guards were gathered to discuss why five of their fellow soldiers had been put to death. One of the soldiers said, "Each guard is required to give his superior a report concerning what, if anything, occurred that was unusual on their watch."

"What are you saying?" another responded. "Have the reports been read?"

Janus, the captain, responded, "The reports of the five guards on duty the night the robbery occurred had nothing in them that explained why such an aggressive act could have taken place without them noticing." Janus pointed his finger at Markus, one of the guards, and said, "I want all the guards that were on duty at other stations that night questioned, and all of their reports read as well. Markus will be in charge of this detail, and you will obey his orders as if they were mine. I will give you a written order that you can present to all of the other guards so they will know their obligation to respond to your questions."

With the authoritative papers provided, Markus began to

interview his fellow soldiers. He thought of the five soldiers that had lost their lives for allowing the deed to take place. He had known all of them well, and wished he could have talked with them about the incident, but he had been told they had been thoroughly questioned and none of them could explain how the thief accomplished his task. Markus thought that meant they were not on their posts, and were not alert.

CHAPTER SEVENTEEN

The garden in the valley was partially hidden by trees and mountains. Hanan was tilling the soil. He was proud of his sweating and digging. It felt good to work for the things he and his mother needed. Despite his burgeoning sense of self-confidence and security, though, he was nagged by worries that the Roman soldiers might ride through their encampment.

That night there was a fire in the large stone fire ring, and it was used to cook the food and to provide warmth against the chilly night air. It was such a joy to see the children running and playing. Their singing was indeed music to Hanan's ears.

Matthias came and sat by Hanan. "How goes it, Hanan? How was your day in the field?"

"It was good, Matthias. I really enjoyed being with everyone, and it is a good feeling to be tired from a day's work. Matthias, have you ever seen the Roman soldiers out here?"

"Yes, Hanan, they do come occasionally, but so far they have left us alone. They appreciate that they do not have to work in the fields because of the vegetables and fish we take to the governor. They also enjoy knowing where we are and that we are not a threat to their authority."

"What about Jesus and His following?" Hanan asked.

"Hanan, most of the crowd that is following Jesus are expecting Him to set up His kingdom here on Earth and overthrow the Roman rulers. We have heard Jesus say, 'My kingdom is not of this world.' The crowd that is following Him has deaf ears to Jesus's message. We have learned that John the Baptist has been beheaded. Jesus Himself is saying that He too will die, but in three days He will rise again. It is sad, but I feel it is true. He will sacrifice His life to pay for all of our sins. I do not understand it all, but in my heart I believe it to be true. I believe God sent His Son to die for us, for there is nothing clean and pure that man can give as an offering."

"Do you mean like Lazarus, Jesus will rise from the grave?"

"Yes, Hanan. You know about Lazarus?"

"I was there," stammered Hanan. "I mean, I watched from a distance. It was so awesome. How will Jesus die, Matthias?"

"Considering the way they took John the Baptist's life, I don't believe it will be gentle. Jesus has far more followers than John the Baptist, and I have learned that it is troublesome news all the way to Herod."

CHAPTER EIGHTEEN

Markus had interviewed most of the guards that were on duty the night of the robbery. He called for another guard who was on duty that night, though his post was nowhere near the dwelling that was invaded. The guard's name was Darius and he stood before Markus at ease. Markus told Darius to have a seat.

Darius hesitated and rudely asked, "How can you give me orders when we are the same rank?"

Markus gruffly replied, "I have my written orders from the captain of the guard, and it would be wise for you to cooperate fully. Now sit down!"

Darius sat down and started to say something else, but Marcus ordered him to be quiet and to just answer the questions.

"Yes, yes, yes sir."

"Good, let us begin. First of all, do you know about the robbery at the dwelling of the governor's aide?"

"Why yes, every one of us is aware of the deed. I knew all of the guards put to death. They were friends of mine."

"Were you near that dwelling that night?"

"No, sir, I—"

"You do not have to call me 'sir,' for as you say, we are of the same rank. Continue."

"My post is the river walk. I patrol a perimeter of two square miles, and part of my patrol is near the river."

"Darius, I have not read your report for that night, but could you tell me anything that you encountered that was unusual?"

"Well, no. Everything was pretty quiet and—wait, yes there was an encounter on my watch. I came alongside the river walk and there was this young man splashing in the water."

"What do you mean by 'splashing'?"

"He was naked and he was washing his garments in the water. He also had a pretty nasty cut on his chest."

"How did he receive the cut on his chest?"

"I don't know."

"You mean you didn't ask him how he was injured. Why?"

"I just didn't think it was necessary."

"It should have been necessary, Darius. Was there anything else you saw that you failed to ask about?"

"No!" Darius answered sharply.

Markus was really disturbed that he was dealing with such incompetency as he asked, "Is this the only encounter you have had with this man?"

Darius began to sweat and fear gripped his heart as he realized that this was not the only time he had seen the man. Dare he lie? No, he decided to tell all he knew and trust in his comrade's mercy. "I saw this same man again another night at the river as I patrolled the area. As I was approaching the man, I saw him toss something into the water."

"What was it he tossed into the water?"

"I could not tell, but I asked him. He said he was fishing and had tossed in a net, but that it got away from him. I also noticed he had a limp when he walked."

"Okay, Darius, was there anything else that you saw?"

"That was the only unusual thing I saw during my patrol."

"Darius, I'm going to ask you the big question. What was the man's name?"

"Well, I—I don't remember his name."

"Darius, if I look at your report will I see the man's name recorded?"

Darius was thinking about his fellow guards that lost their lives because of their neglect and became very nervous.

"I asked you a question: do you remember writing the man's name in your report?"

Darius could not lie and get away with it because he knew the man's name would not be in the report. He finally blurted out, "I did not get his name!"

There was a period of silence as Markus walked away. He was upset at what he had just heard. "Darius, do you realize the predicament you will be in if this man is found guilty of a crime?"

"I am so sorry. Please help me. I beg of you."

Markus felt sorry for the soldier, but also realized he could not hide Darius's slackness of duty. "Darius, I am doing my duty and I must report all my findings to my captain. I will not falsify a report. And he is most assuredly going to want the name of this man you saw. He will have to make the decision concerning your discipline."

Darius suddenly remembered the man that some of the guards had brought into the jail a night ago. He told Marcus, "I think I may have more information for you to think about."

"Yes, go on."

"Well, I was coming off duty a night ago; this man was brought to the jail. I recognized him. I know his name. His name is Shiam. He runs a small trading shop. I have been in his place. He has mostly junk. I don't see why anyone would buy from him."

"What has this man Shiam got to do with the man with no name?"

Darius wished he had made the connection that night at the river, but he had it now.

"This man in the water I saw, he would hardly be recognizable, for he was wet and unseemly."

"Make your point, Darius."

"I remember now. I have seen the same man I saw in the river go into Shiam's place before. It was nighttime, but I still remember seeing him go into the shop."

Markus was almost at a loss for words, as he realized how careless Darius was as a sentry.

"Darius, I'm going to try to find out the name of the man you saw in the river. If I do, I will present it in the report I give the captain. However, I will not enter the name on your report. If I find out the name, you should be all right; if not, you will have to present yourself to the captain. You may just have saved your life, Darius."

Darius left his meeting with Markus with mixed emotions. He fretted over possibly having to face the captain and, at the same time, hoped Markus would find the man's name and protect him. He thought that Markus seemed like a good soldier and he would find the right man. He also felt bad, as he realized his mistake.

CHAPTER NINETEEN

Matthias was excited as he approached Hanan and his mother along the pathway.

"Hanan, Eunice, Jesus is on his way back to Nazareth and we can go see Him as He passes through our village. Come, let us go quickly. We must not miss seeing Him."

Hanan held on to his mother as he helped her along the way. They had not traveled long before they came upon a group of people. The people were angry and held stones in their hand. "She has sinned!" the crowd yelled. "Let us stone her to death!"

Coming closer to the crowd they saw Jesus.

Hanan recognized Jesus immediately, by His countenance and His voice.

The yelling stopped, and it was very quiet as the group waited for Jesus to speak.

"Ye who are without sin cast the first stone."

Hanan could hear the sound of rocks dropping to the ground.

Jesus asked the woman, "Where are your accusers?"

The woman replied, "There are none."

Jesus said, "Neither do I condemn thee. Go and sin no more."

"What a beautiful experience!" Hanan's mother said. "Hanan, I want to know more about Jesus."

So they joined the crowd that was walking behind Jesus. Hanan stayed with his mother and some other older people, who could not keep up with Jesus and those who walked ahead.

When they reached the lake where a crowd was gathered around Jesus, Hanan sought a vantage point where they could see Jesus better. When he turned, he saw that his mother was not by him. As he looked in all directions for his mother, he saw her standing directly in front of Jesus. He pushed through the crowd until he was as close as he could get to Jesus. There she was—his mother was being touched by Jesus, and she had a radiance he had never seen before. Then he remembered: "Yes, I have seen that glow! The woman who touched the hem of His garment that day had the same radiance around her."

Hanan was drawn to go to ask Jesus to touch him, forgive him of his wrongs, like He had the woman who was almost stoned to death, but he felt unclean as he watched his mother glow and he felt the shame he had inside.

Hanan walked with his mother back to their dwelling. When they were inside, Hanan's mother said, "Hanan, it has been such a glorious day. I will never be the same again. I have met my Savior. I am ready to go be with your father, Nathan. I must lie down now. Hanan, I love you and our Savior loves you. I want you to find Him and let Him bless you. I will lie down now and sleep peacefully."

"I love you too, Mother, and I have made up my mind to seek Jesus and ask Him to bless me. I want to go to heaven and live with God and our family."

Hanan sat and watched his mother sleeping. She still had a glow about her. Hanan thought, *I must find Jesus and confess my wrongdoing and ask for forgiveness.*

He lay across his bed and was soon asleep. When he awoke, he felt a peace that he had never experienced before.

Hanan stood up and headed out of the house, but he looked down and saw the cloth ties that he had wrapped around his sandals. They had pulled loose. Ever since the night he left his sandals while he was stealing the gold necklace, he had to wear these worn-out ones.

Hanan walked towards the lake. He soon found himself on top of a crest and he sat on one of the large stones. He looked down to where Jesus had been and relived the experience of seeing his mother receive blessings from Jesus. Hanan was feeling so at peace and thought all was good for him and his mother.

Hanan heard his name being called and he stood up to see who might be yelling for him. He suddenly heard his name called again. This time it was much closer. He turned and looked and he saw Matthias waving. Matthias was beckoning for him to come down from the hilltop.

"What is wrong, Matthias?" Hanan asked when he came closer. "You seem anxious. Are the soldiers harassing our community?"

"No, Hanan, it's Eunice. Amon and I went to see her and take her some food. We did not get a response when we knocked on the door and called her name. Hanan, your mother has joined your father in heaven. We entered the house and found her in her bed. She had a beautiful smile on her face."

Hanan began to weep out loud and he choked while saying, "Matthias, she was so happy that she had met Jesus, and I know she believed He was the Son of God."

Matthias smiled as he said, "Hanan, she was right. The man we call Jesus is God's Son sent to this world to be our Savior. Many of my friends believe Jesus to be the Messiah. They thought He would take down the Roman Empire and rule as king on this Earth. They have had a difficult time accepting His saying, 'My kingdom is not of this world.'"

They were walking towards home and after a period of silence, Hanan asked, "Matthias, explain to me why this Jesus with all of His powers is not on Earth to be our king."

"Hanan, it has been some time since we first began providing burnt offerings for our sins, but man truly does not have anything clean enough to offer as a sacrifice. Jesus is our king and we should accept him as our king, but he is building a place in heaven for those who follow Him. That is where your mother is now. She is waiting for us to join her. You witnessed your mother accepting Jesus as Savior and Lord."

They were almost home as Hanan said, "Matthias, I don't understand why John the Baptist was killed. He was a good man. I truly don't understand why Jesus should have to die. I have seen Him perform many miracles, including the raising of Lazarus from the grave."

"He could surely avoid being killed at the hands of man, but it is for us He has come, that we may be saved. He has said, 'No man cometh unto the Father except by Me.' We saw with our own eyes as Lazarus was raised from the grave. Surely there is no grave that can hold the one who gives life to others."

Matthias placed his hand on Hanan's shoulder as they both knelt by the bedside of Hanan's mother. Matthias began to pray, "Oh merciful God, our Creator and heavenly Father. We kneel by our beloved Eunice; welcome her into Your kingdom. Thank You, Lord, for providing a way for us to come unto You. Be with my friend Hanan, comfort him and lead him to Jesus your Son where he can find complete release from his sorrow and his sins."

All of the community came together as Hanan's mother was laid to rest. Hanan felt the love of everyone, as they poured out their hearts to support him. Hanan was sorrowful and did not work in the fields for several days, but he soon went back to tilling the soil and found release as he worked in the sun and sweated. He thought of his father as he worked the land. He could feel his body becoming stronger, and his soul was becoming more at rest.

∞ ∞ ∞

Shiam's cell door opened and he saw the face of a new Roman soldier. He drew back in a corner and cried out, "Please don't hit me anymore! Why am I being tortured this way?"

Markus had read the report turned in by the guards who took Shiam to the jail. According to the report, a traveler had been stopped and searched. They found a bar of gold in his belongings. They questioned how he had obtained the gold. The traveler told them that he couldn't refuse the gold at the price at which it was offered. With further questioning, the traveler told the soldiers he had purchased the gold from Shiam.

CHAPTER TWENTY

Matthias and Hanan were up early, as they wanted to go see one of Matthias's friends, who lived with his wife and four children closer towards Nazareth. The friend, Ulstra, had barely escaped being killed by the Roman soldiers a short while back. He had argued with one of the soldiers. Before they could put their hands on him, though, he had escaped. He lived with a fear that he and his family would be found, fearing they would be killed. He also knew Matthias and the others were risking their lives by harboring them.

After Matthias and Hanan had traveled over some rocky, barren land for quite a while, Matthias stopped. "You wait here, Hanan. I need to locate Ulstra and assure him you are a friend. He is suspicious of any new faces."

Hanan sat upon a large stone and looked in the valley below. He grew angry as he thought about how so many of his people lived in fear of the Romans.

Matthias returned with Ulstra and introduced the men. Hanan could see clearly why Ulstra would be a good friend.

Ulstra was a tall man and very thin, with large hands roughened by work. With a big smile on his face, Ulstra said, "Come, come see my family. You are welcome here."

They went into a cave in the mountain. Once Hanan had adjusted his eyes to the darkness, he saw five other smiling faces as the light from the oil lamp shone on them.

"My name is Hanan, and I come in peace. We have brought you food and oil. I'm sorry you have to live this way and have to hide from the Romans."

"We are blessed by the Lord our God," said Ulstra. "I have my family and I have Matthias as a friend."

They visited for a while longer, and then Ulstra said, "Down by the lake earlier today we all stood behind the stones and looked below to see a crowd by the lake. There was a man talking to the group gathered there. We saw him heal people with all kinds of afflictions. We wondered who the man could be. Have you ever heard about him?"

Hanan responded so quickly he surprised himself. "The man is called Jesus. I've seen Him perform all manner of miracles." Hanan told them about the miracle of turning the water into wine, the woman who touched the hem of His garment and the raising of Lazarus from the dead. Ulstra seemed to be in a daze listening to Hanan's words and said, "And you have met this man called Jesus?"

Hanan thought about the times he had seen Jesus, always from a distance. He also thought about his life, as he answered, "No, I have not personally met Jesus, but I've seen from afar with my own eyes these things." Hanan hesitated but added, "My mother experienced the healing power of this Jesus, and she was convinced that Jesus is the Messiah sent by God."

CHAPTER TWENTY-ONE

Shiam continued to cower in the corner of his cell, begging Markus to please not beat him anymore.

"Here, get to your feet!" Markus had taken hold of Shiam and helped him up. Markus felt pity for the prisoner Shiam and thought he lived no better than a rat. Markus decided to take Shiam out of his cell to where he would be more comfortable as he questioned him. He thought that some food and a little sunshine would cause Shiam to answer his questions more freely. He led Shaim into another room and told him to have a seat. He asked the guard to bring food and drink for the prisoner.

The guard resisted. "You have no authority over me, and why waste food on this weasel?"

"You will do as ordered or explain your actions to the captain. Now what is it going to be—food and drink or the captain? One more thing, bring water and a washcloth for the prisoner to wash before he eats his meal."

The guard did not answer Markus as he abruptly left the room. Markus waited to talk to Shiam and looked over the notes he had taken thus far concerning the robbery.

Shiam sat with his hands over his face and waited with anticipation for food and drink. The door opened, and the guard with the food came and placed it all on the small table along with the washcloth and basin of water.

"That will be all," Markus told the guard.

"But I am supposed to remain with the prisoner," said the guard.

Markus showed his anger as he shouted, "I have a written order from the captain. If I have any more trouble, you will become a prisoner yourself. Now leave at once!"

The guard made a quick exit and Markus turned to observe his prisoner, Shiam. He had not taken time to wash before eating and food mingled with the dirt on his face and hands.

Markus was overcome with dislike but also compassion for this man. "Shiam, take the cloth and wash yourself."

Shiam scrubbed his face and washed his hands and his feet. When he was finished with the washcloth, he dropped it into the dirty water. He had a grin on his face as he said, "I have never stolen anything from any of you Romans. I do not deserve to be treated with such abuse."

Markus paused and then replied, "Shiam, I don't believe you stole the item we are concerned about, but I don't believe you are completely innocent. How did you acquire the gold you sold to the traveler?"

Shiam felt some relief as he thought, *They are not questioning me about that valuable item Hanan last brought to me.*

He took a while to answer Marcus's question. "I have traded things I have for small gold nuggets, and when I have enough, I melt them down into a bar of gold I can sell."

Marcus was amazed at how convincing Shiam's story unfolded, but he also knew that he was lying. He decided not to mention the governor's ceremonial necklace right away. "Do you have the names of those you have done business with?"

Shiam did know some of the people, and he thought he would be set free if he gave Markus a name. "The traveler you mention has been to my shop many times. His name is Anthony."

Shiam realized the soldiers had already obtained the name from the traveler, and thought his giving Markus the name would go well for his release from jail.

But Markus decided to ask a question for which he himself did not have an answer. He realized this was not a favorable position, but he asked, "Shiam, I'm sure you have heard about someone stealing a valuable gold necklace that belonged to the governor."

Shiam felt he was losing all he had gained with his previous answer to Markus's question. He became very nervous and hid his face in his hands. If he told the truth, he knew it would lead to Hanan. If he lied, he could face harsher punishment. Shiam hesitated too long.

"Shiam, it is not a difficult question. Do you know anyone who may have been involved in this crime?"

Shiam thought if they found he was involved they would kill him. He felt it was possible he could lie and get away with it. He cleared his throat and said, "I have heard about the crime, but I know no one who would be guilty of such a crime." He hoped they did not already know anything about Hanan, who was the only person who could connect him with the jeweled necklace.

Markus realized Shiam had established a barrier with his answer, so he decided to be less accommodating with the rest of his questions.

CHAPTER TWENTY-TWO

Hanan was on his way to see Amon. He had to tell him the truth concerning how he had lived his life as a thief. It would be a hard thing for him to do, but it had to be done. Hanan thought, *Will I lose the community's friendship? Will they cast me out from their presence?* Hanan thought about his mother, and was thankful she had not found out about his life as a thief.

Amon welcomed Hanan with a hug and a kiss on his cheek. "Come, my brother, it is always a joy to see you. Is there anything you need? I know you are grieving, but one day we will all rejoice together again."

"Thank you, Amon, you are a dear friend, and I so appreciate your kindness to my mother. I do have a need this day, but it is not one for food or substance. It is a far greater need than for things."

"What might that be, Hanan? I will do my best to help you."

"Amon, you and Matthias, as well as everyone else here, have been such a blessing to me and my mother. I have lived a lie for so long. I've lived it ever since I have been old enough to provide for my mother. I am so thankful that my mother was spared the knowledge that her son was a thief." Hanan paused to see how what he had just said was affecting Amon.

Amon broke the silence. "Go ahead, Hanan. Speak what's bothering you. I will be prayerfully listening."

"Amon, I started when I was very young. The Romans had killed my father, and I developed anger in my heart towards them. I stole only from the Romans, and only to provide food and sustenance for my mother. I was good at stealing things and my mother was so proud of me for being the man of the house. I guess it happens to most all thieves, we get greedy, and go for bigger rewards." Hanan told Amon the complete story about his life as a thief.

Amon stood up, his back towards Hanan. He finally turned around and said, "Hanan, what you have done and what you have been come as a surprise to me, as I'm sure it will to the rest of the community. However, our heavenly Father forgives us of our sins when we offer our best for a sacrifice on the altar. You have seen Jesus, as you say, from afar, but still you have seen Him heal, cleanse and forgive others. You must believe He will also heal, cleanse and forgive you as well."

Hanan felt a sense of joy as he listened to Amon speak, but then he wondered what the rest of the community would think. "Amon, the last item I took belonged to the governor, and soldiers are searching for it. If they find out who stole it, they will put him to death. I have faced that possibility throughout my life, but I feel anyone who hides a thief from the Romans will be killed also. I do not want to bring trouble to your family and the others."

Hanan waited for Amon's response, concerned that his friend was going to lash out at him. Amon himself had successfully escaped the hands of the Roman soldiers. Amon said, "Hanan, this is trouble indeed, and what has been done we cannot undo. You're surely correct when you say whoever is found guilty of this offense will be put to death. I also believe if it is discovered that you lived among us, we will not be dealt with gently. You are right to bring this to the attention of our community. I cannot answer for everyone, but it is my prayer that we will be led by the Lord to do what is right regarding this situation. Have you told Matthias or anyone else about this?"

"No, I have not, Amon. I thought you were the first I should talk with, as you yourself have experienced a little elusiveness regarding the Romans."

"You're correct in what you say, Hanan, but I cannot make the decision for the community. I will talk to Matthias and the others. We will all pray for God's guidance. I think you should seek to find Jesus as expediently as possible. We have provided a physical hedge around you, but He will provide you a spiritual fortress against the enemy."

CHAPTER TWENTY-THREE

Shiam had just told Markus that he did not know any details about the robbery of the gold necklace, and also that he did not know anyone involved with the crime.

Markus decided to get tougher with the questioning. "Shiam, the traveler we caught with the bar of gold stated he had purchased gold from you several times at an unheard of price. We're going to stop with your lies and ridiculous answers to my questions. We have searched your place you call a shop, and there is nothing of value there. In fact, it is a rat-infested pigsty. It is obvious you have nothing of value to sell, yet you still have money to buy gold. That leaves only one other way you could obtain this amount of gold, and that would be by stealing it from someone. Have you been stealing the gold from anyone, Shiam? Before you answer the question, I want you to know that I mean directly or indirectly stealing. We did find a smelting pot and a casting mold inside your place. I suspect you have been melting down stolen gold. Am I right?"

Shiam realized he was cornered. He also knew he would not be released from the jail. He now wished he had told Markus the truth. If he had been truthful from the start he believed he would have probably received some mercy from Markus. Markus seemed like a fair man and a soldier of honor. He knew now that the truth would not have the same effect. He also knew he would have to be convincing and hope Markus would show some mercy.

"Yes, you are right. I did receive items from people who wanted to get rid of them quickly and I knew they were stolen."

Markus felt he was getting closer to finding out about the governor's missing necklace and pushed Shiam even harder. "Do you want to change your story about the missing gold necklace belonging to the governor?"

Shiam was now very nervous. He was wringing his hands as he hesitantly said, "I did see the gold necklace. It was brought into my shop." Shiam knew he was in deep trouble regardless of what he now said, so he decided to stretch the truth and hope to gain some ground with Markus.

He continued. "Someone brought the necklace into my shop, but I sent the man away. I told him I did not want to have anything to do with the necklace." Shiam breathed a sigh of relief that he had made his case regarding the necklace.

But Marcus continued, asking him, "What was the name of the man who brought the necklace to your shop?"

Shiam felt anger overtake him as he thought about Hanan and that cursed gold necklace.

If I give Markus Hanan's name, Hanan will be captured, and tell the Romans the truth, which would be different from my story.

Shiam said, "I do not know the man's name."

CHAPTER TWENTY-FOUR

Hanan left Amon's home with mixed emotions. He was glad he had told Amon, and thus the community, about living the life of a thief. His heart was also heavy, having brought his problem to people who had been so generous with love to him and his mother. He hoped his actions would not bring soldiers to the community as they searched for him. Hanan was now determined to try to find Jesus and ask for His blessings. He had felt so clean and free from fear while living among the families in the community. Now that he had revealed his troubles to the community that had been so benevolent to him, the fear and shame were once again upon him. He wondered where he could find Jesus as he started out to do just that.

CHAPTER TWENTY-FIVE

Markus had been questioning Shiam for hours, and he knew Shiam was becoming weak and almost falling asleep where he sat. Markus realized he too was tired, and although it may not be aggressive enough in the eyes of some to ease off on Shiam, Markus made the decision to end the questioning and treat the prisoner humanely. "Shiam, that will be all for today, but I will be back. Until I return, you will be treated well."

He called the guard. "This prisoner is to be fed properly and given water to bathe himself each day. There are to be no beatings given this man. You are to give this information to all of the other guards."

The guard objected to Markus's orders and said so, but he was reprimanded.

"You have been given orders that are as strong as if the captain gave them in person. I will be back to question the prisoner again. Take him to his cell!"

Shiam was glad the questioning was over, and he was so glad to hear the orders to the guard. He now would have time to think about how he was going to handle questions when Markus returned.

∞∞∞∞

It was a new day and Markus was staring out of the window of the guards' quarters, thinking about the assignment he had been given.

He decided to ride to the post of each of the guards. He wanted to know if any of them had any new information regarding the robbery.

Markus had covered all the posts but one. The post remaining was the post that covered the area by the river. As he approached, he recognized the guard on duty as Darius.

"Welcome to my watch, Markus."

"Thank you, Darius. How goes it with you? Have you any news regarding the robbery?"

"No news, Markus, all is quiet on my watch."

"Carry on, Darius. I will not keep you from your assignment."

Markus decided to ride alongside the river. He knew the river well. He often came to the river to meditate on his problems. He remembered a favorite spot along the river and rode towards the often-visited location.

CHAPTER TWENTY-SIX

Hanan walked towards the city of Jerusalem in search of Jesus. He began his journey with his mind filled with the loss of his mother, and the regret of having to leave Matthias and all the people who had befriended him. His quest to find Jesus gave him hope, but he also feared that this was his last chance to find the Savior and receive a blessing like his mother had experienced. He asked people along the way if they knew where Jesus could be found, but none of those he talked with knew the whereabouts of Jesus.

"Good morning," he said to an older man and his wife as he caught up with them on the road. "I'm trying to find the man who has been preaching and healing many people. His name is Jesus. Have you seen Him?"

"I have heard of Him," the man replied, "but have not heard any fresh news the past couple of days. It seems that all people want to talk about is the search for the thief who stole the gold necklace from the governor."

This caused Hanan's fear to increase and he wondered if he could allude the soldiers long enough to find Jesus. One man told Hanan that the Romans had arrested a man called Shiam and that they had him in the jail. The news of Shiam's capture upset Hanan, as he wondered what Shiam had told his captors. He felt he was closer to being arrested, and what he really wanted was to be close to the man called Jesus.

Once Hanan was in Jerusalem, the activity of the people rushing to and fro caused him to think of the peaceful community he had enjoyed with Matthias and Amon. As he tried to ask about Jesus, he was pushed aside by the hurrying crowd. No one knew where Jesus was, and Hanan's question seemed to agitate the people he questioned. He saw a man sitting on a bench by himself. Hanan approached the man and asked, "May I join you for a while?"

"Yes," the man replied, "I could use some company right now. My name is Ramon. What is your name?"

"My name is Hanan and I am trying to find the man called Jesus. Do you know where I could find Him?"

Ramon was not agitated by the question but rather smiled as he answered, "No, I don't know where He is but you are not the only one looking for Him. He has the temple leaders very upset, and when they get upset the Roman rulers want to silence whoever is causing the disturbance."

"Why would the temple leaders be angry with Jesus?"

"Jesus has claimed to be the Son of God and the leader of the people. Neither the temple leaders nor the Romans like to hear of anyone expressing authority over them. The Romans are already aggressive and angry because of someone stealing something from them. They have searched and plundered many homes trying to find a valuable piece of jewelry. I pity the man who stole it if they ever find him."

The words of the man caused Hanan's heart to beat fast and he wondered, *Will they arrest Jesus or me first?*

"Thank you for sharing your bench and your time, Ramon."

After he told Ramon farewell, Hanan proceeded on his journey seeking Jesus.

CHAPTER TWENTY-SEVEN

Markus had arrived at his favorite place along the river. He dismounted and walked towards the rocky area, where the water was shallow. He sat down on the rocky slope and looked over the water. He thought of his homeland and the Jewish people the Romans ruled over. He thought of how it would be to go home to his land and let these humble people live in peace.

As his eyes wandered on the river, something shining in the shallow water caught his attention. This was an area where things washed ashore, becoming tangled with the weeds and grasses. He stood up and looked at the object that had gained his attention and waded into the gentle flow. The bright daylight caused the object to look like the image of the sun itself as it glistened. He reached into the water to retrieve the object, but it was entangled and did not pull free. He stood erect and looked towards the shining object again, but he had stirred up the water, which was now muddy and cloudy. After the water had cleared, Markus reached with both hands and jerked on the heavy piece. It broke loose and he fell backwards into the water with the weighty object on his chest.

Lifting himself out of the water, Markus looked at the trophy he had found. He could not believe what his eyes beheld! It was the governor's ceremonial gold necklace. So much anger and death had happened because of this weed-infested jewel, and holding it in his hands caused Markus to be elated and weary at the same time. He cleaned it off and headed back to where his horse was waiting.

CHAPTER TWENTY-EIGHT

After Amon told Matthias about Hanan's revelations, they set up a meeting with the community leaders. Matthias stood before the people and informed them about Hanan.

Matthias said, "It is with a heavy heart I stand before you this day. Our brother Hanan is facing some real hardships. Hanan took seriously his responsibility to provide for his mother. All of you know Hanan lost his father to the Roman soldiers, and to provide for her he resorted to taking things from the Romans. Hanan loved his mother and she was so pleased when they became a part of our community. Hanan did not want to bring trouble to us. He knew the soldiers would be looking for him, and he did not want them to find him here. I must tell you, we can expect the soldiers to visit us if they do not find Hanan in and around the city. You will be asked questions by the soldiers, and you must tell the truth. Hanan did dwell among us for a while, but we do not know where he is now. Hanan is searching for Jesus. We have all seen the miracles of Jesus. We have witnessed His healing and love. The Healer that Hanan is searching for is Himself now being sought. I fear He will be treated as John the Baptist was treated. I don't understand why Jesus does not destroy His foe, but He seems to be placing Himself like a lamb to slaughter. Let us pray for Hanan that he will find Jesus. Let us also pray for Jesus, God's sent Savior."

He concluded his remarks by saying, "Let us all remember what Jesus said to the woman that was about to be stoned to death because of her sins. I repeat His words to you this day: 'Ye who are without sin cast the first stone.'"

The people agreed that they should pray for Hanan, and if he should happen to return, they would welcome him. They also agreed that if the soldiers should come and question them, they could truthfully say they did not know where Hanan was. Amon led them all in a prayer for their friend.

CHAPTER TWENTY-NINE

Markus stood by his horse holding the gold necklace. It was heavy, and he thought of how daring it was for someone to accomplish the task of stealing the necklace. He threw the trophy in his pouch and rode off towards the guards' quarters and Captain Janus. He had the governor's necklace, but he was sure they would still insist on finding the thief to punish him. Markus wished he could return the necklace to the governor, release Shiam from jail, and forget about finding the one who stole the necklace. He had never met the thief, but he felt like he knew him, and was developing a respect for one who could successfully steal the gold necklace without being caught. Markus knew there was a connection between the man and Shiam and he intended to find out when he questioned Shiam again.

After the captain heard of the recovery of the ceremonial necklace from Markus and shared the information with the governor, he called together the other Roman soldiers to announce the news.

"This has been a successful mission brought about mostly by the excellent work of Markus. I have selected him to be second in command. You will all take your orders from him. The governor is very pleased that the jewel stolen from him has been recovered, but he is still adamant about finding the one who committed the crime."

When they were all dismissed, Markus asked Darius to remain. "Darius, I wanted you to know that your recollection of the event with the man in the water led us to finding the necklace. I also want you to know you have nothing hanging over you. I will favor you in my report."

Darius was overwhelmed by what Markus told him. "Thank you, Markus. I will do my best to prove you can have confidence in me from this day forward."

When Markus arrived back at the jail, he did not go to Shiam's cell, but rather instructed the guard to go and get Shiam. "Bring Shiam to me, and for your sake, I don't want to see any evidence of abuse."

Word had traveled quickly of Markus's advancement in rank and authority, so the guards prepared the prisoner Shiam so he would show well to Markus. The guard entered the room with Shiam in front of him.

"That will be all," Markus told the guard. He turned to Shiam, who looked clean and alert. "Have a seat, Shiam. Have you been treated well since my last visit?"

"Thanks to you I have been treated much better, but I feel I should be set free. I have answered all of your questions."

Markus felt better questioning Shiam, seeing he was better mentally and physically. Markus paused before saying, "Shiam, you must be entirely truthful with me. We have recovered the gold necklace."

Markus was careful not to tell Shiam where they had found the stolen property, as he wanted Shiam to reveal the name of the man who had brought it to him.

"Shiam, now that we have the necklace and know about the thief, we need you to give us the name of the thief to confirm our information."

Shiam still thought he would never be released from jail, regardless of what he told Markus. He had heard about the guards who allowed the robbery to take place being killed. *Why would they not do the same to me?* Shiam asked himself. He wanted to purchase as much time as he could to stay alive. *Where did they find the necklace? Was it at Hanan's home? Hanan, would not keep it there,* Shiam reasoned. He believed Hanan must have put it somewhere and the soldiers had found the necklace, but not Hanan.

It seemed like hours since he heard Markus ask for the name of the thief, but it had only been several minutes. Shiam decided to try to buy more time by risking another lie: "As I have already told you, I do not know his name."

Shiam's answer disappointed Marcus, but he realized he had not found the necklace with anyone, but rather in the river. Shiam did not know this, but Markus believed he took a chance by answering the question as he did. Markus was running out of questions to ask Shiam, so he used his last option.

"Shiam, you disappoint me. I was hoping you would answer by telling the truth. I have a witness who saw the man we are looking for enter and exit your shop, and it was late at night. What kind of business do you do in the dark of night?"

Shiam wondered if Markus had Hanan's name, or if they had just seen Hanan but did not know who he was. He also thought it was night, and they possibly did not really see Hanan clearly. Shiam also realized that if he supplied Hanan's name, Hanan would make it the end of any defense he might have. He decided to continue and said, "I have many people who visit often in the night. I do not know the name of the man you are searching for."

Markus realized he had reached the end of questioning Shiam.

"Shiam, I have no more questions at this time, but I'm sure I will have more evidence the next time we meet. You will not be able to lie anymore and separate yourself from the crime against the governor."

Markus wondered if the truth would come forth if he let the guards be harsher with Shiam. He considered it for a moment but decided to find the truth himself.

Shiam asked, "Am I going to be free to go?"

Markus replied, "No, Shiam, you will stay here until we solve this mystery. You'll be given an opportunity to face the truth, and I assure you, it will be uncovered."

With that, Marcus summoned the guard to take Shiam back to his cell.

CHAPTER THIRTY

Hanan was continuing his search for Jesus in Jerusalem, but fearful of being discovered and arrested. In his quest for information, he was told once again that the Romans had a man in custody by the name of Shiam and that Shiam was accused of robbing the Roman government. He also learned that they were looking for another man who was involved in the crime. Hanan knew he was the one they were looking for and was somewhat relieved that those he spoke to did not mention his name.

Hanan met a man who was begging for money. Hanan reached in his cloak and pulled out all the money he had and gave it to the beggar. He thought about how he himself almost became a beggar. He also felt his life was coming to an end. Hanan realized he could not go back and live in the community with Amon and Matthias. He did not want to cause hardship to those who had been so good to him and his mother.

Hanan asked the beggar, "Have you seen the man called Jesus?"

The beggar withdrew and seemed to be alarmed by Hanan's question. "I know nothing about this man you call Jesus. I am not one of His followers! Leave me be!"

A man who had observed the encounter with the beggar placed a hand on Hanan's shoulder and said, "You have frightened the one who begs. He does not want to be identified with Jesus because the soldiers are searching to find Him. He has caused even more disturbances than the one they called John the Baptist. If Jesus is found, He will surely meet the same fate. No one wants to proclaim any allegiance to Jesus. They fear they will be treated harshly if they are seen as followers."

Hanan thought, *I'm running away from capture just like Jesus.*

He wished for their paths to cross. He knew that if he met Jesus again he would ask for the same blessing that had been given his mother. Hanan found a stable and decided to make it his home for the night.

CHAPTER THIRTY-ONE

Janus had called Markus in for an update on the pursuit of the thief.

"Markus, are you sure the man we have in our jail is not the thief?"

"Janus," he said to his captain, "I am absolutely sure this man Shiam could not have accomplished such a feat, but I am equally sure he is involved in some way with the man who did the robbery."

"Has this man Shiam given you the name of the thief?"

"No, but I think he feels as long as he withholds the name, he will prolong being punished. Once we have the name, he will not be of any value to us."

"Markus, perhaps you are being a little too kind to our prisoner. I know you have a big heart as well as a good mind. That's why I have chosen you to be my second in command. But you can delegate to others to be more forceful in interrogating our prisoner."

Markus replied, "I will obey what orders you give me. You know I will. I'm asking for just a little more time to try the plan I have for capturing the man who stole the governor's necklace."

"Very well, Markus, I'll grant you your request, but if we are not closer to solving this issue when we meet again, the prisoner will be forced to reveal the man's name."

"Thank you, Janus. I know you are being questioned by the government. I will find the man and bring him to you very soon."

"You're right, Markus. I have to listen to my superiors as they accuse me of being incompetent to solve this matter. They too are questioning our leniency with the prisoner. You're a good soldier, Markus, and I'll give you this last chance to use your heart and mind to find this man. If you fail in your endeavor, we will take a harsher course."

CHAPTER THIRTY-TWO

In the Garden of Gethsemane, Jesus was praying. He had instructed His disciples to pray also, but they were tired and could not resist the body's call for sleep.

There were only eleven disciples with Jesus that night in the garden. Judas's absence was especially noteworthy because the Teacher had accused him of betrayal during their meal together the previous evening. Judas's absence further confirmed the other disciples' suspicions.

It was as Jesus was praying in the garden that Judas appeared with the Roman soldiers. The disciple walked up to Jesus and kissed Him on the cheek. When Judas stepped away, the soldiers arrested Jesus and carried Him off.

CHAPTER THIRTY-THREE

Markus was not a part of the cadre of the soldiers that arrested Jesus, but he was present when He was brought in to the governor's quarters. Markus felt a strange, uneasy emotion as he looked into the eyes of Jesus. Markus remembered how learning of John the Baptist's beheading had caused him to question how the Roman Empire was treating its subjects, concerns he kept to himself. Markus had heard some of Jesus's speeches and felt He was a man of peace. The thing that caused alarm was the people calling Jesus "king." Markus was glad he was not assigned the order to arrest Jesus, since he had the assignment to catch the thief.

Markus decided he could gain more information by walking among the people as one of them, so he removed his helmet and all of the armor he wore as a soldier and ventured into the streets.

∞∞∞

Hanan watched the soldiers bring the Jesus into town, laughing and treating Him roughly. "Ha, behold your king," one of the soldiers laughed. Let us see what miracles the king will perform for us today!"

One bystander walked up to Jesus and spat upon Him saying, "You are not a king! You are just a troublemaker! They took care of the trouble-making baptizer—now they will take care of you!"

Jesus looked in the eyes of the people in the crowd as He was led down the street. His eyes seem to say, *I love you.* But the eyes of the people, unable to look into the eyes of Jesus, were filled with a mixture of despair and hate.

Hanan's heart felt a sense of grief and he sat down on the side of the pathway. He had the appearance of a beggar as he hung his head in despair. He wondered if Jesus would be treated as John the Baptist was and it caused him to openly weep. Hanan did not know how long he had spent in his sorrowful state when he felt a hand on his shoulder. He looked up to see Matthias staring down at him.

"Hanan, I had to find you. We have all been praying for you. We are grieving over the news of our Savior's arrest by the Romans. Hanan, we are even more grieved by the way the people are turning against Jesus. Those that once followed Jesus expecting Him to become their king are now ridiculing Him."

Matthias helped Hanan to his feet and led him to a building on the edge of town. When they were inside, Matthias led him to an upper room where Amon and Ulstra greeted him with their hugs of love. They had brought food, and Hanan was thankful, as he was indeed hungry.

After finishing his meal Hanan asked, "What is happening? First they killed John the Baptist and now they have Jesus. What will they do with Him? We have all seen the miracles. Why doesn't He use his power to escape from the hands of His captors?"

Matthias answered Hanan: "Hanan, we have a small group that has accepted Jesus's words concerning His purpose on earth. He has said He will die, but in three days rise up from the grave. We believe God sent His only Son to be a sacrifice for all of our sins. We have nothing to sacrifice for our sins. Jesus will suffer death in our place. We are praying that Jesus will not be treated as John the Baptist."

Hanan had tears in his eyes as he haltingly said, "I am so thankful you have brought me food and your prayers mean so much to me. You all have risked danger by being seen with me. I cherish your love and friendship."

"Hanan, we love you and wish we could ease this burden you have upon you," Amon said. "If our prayers will lift the burden, you know you have them."

Matthias agreed. "Hanan, all of the community is praying for you and they send their love."

Hanan said, "I can see you have been blessed by Jesus. It was my hope that I too could receive this blessing. I saw it happen for my mother and I see it in all of you. I do believe Jesus to be the Son of God and although I may not be able to speak to Him or touch Him directly, my soul has a peace as if He has touched me."

Hanan looked deeply into his friends' faces. "They have in custody Shiam, the one to whom I took the things I stole. It's just a matter of time before I am arrested, but because of the peace I feel, I can face what lies ahead for me. Thanks to all of you and take my words of love back to everyone."

CHAPTER THIRTY-FOUR

Inside the leather bag strapped on Markus's shoulder were a piece of torn cloth and a pair of sandals. He walked slowly through the streets, smiling and greeting people along the way, but pondering so many questions. *Why is it so important to find the man who stole the necklace? Why kill a man like John the Baptist? Why arrest the man called Jesus, someone who goes about doing good?*

Markus realized he was thinking like a captive of Rome and forgetting he was a soldier with orders that had to be carried out. When he got to the edge of town, he stopped to think about his next move.

∞ ∞ ∞

Shiam had been treated fairly well since Markus had visited him. In overhearing the guards talk, he learned that the Romans had brought in the man they call Jesus. Shiam knew about Jesus but had never seen him. Everything he'd heard about the man was good and Shiam wondered why they would imprison him. Perhaps Jesus brought too much attention to Himself and it disturbed the Romans. The man did, after all, draw large crowds wherever he was teaching and performed amazing miracles. Shiam realized they probably felt He was a troublemaker.

Shiam was angry with Hanan for all the trouble he had caused him, but continued to think it best if Hanan was never caught.

Once they had Hanan, he believed, his fate would be death by the Romans.

∞∞∞

Markus was about to start back to his quarters when he saw the four men coming out of a building. He looked at each man carefully and suddenly he noticed one of the men had on sandals that were tied with straps of cloth and that he was limping. Marcus walked closer toward the group of men, and then he observed the bright purple patch that had been sewn on the man's cloak. Marcus walked up to the man, and after greeting him he opened his leather bag and withdrew the piece of cloth and pair of sandals. Markus did not say anything, but rather he held the piece of cloth up to Hanan's chest. The piece of cloth matched Hanan's patched cloak. Markus then held out the pair of sandals and ask Hanan, "You look like you could use some sandals. Are these yours?"

Hanan realized it was over for him, and he asked Markus if his friends could leave. Markus was certain he had his thief and also felt the other three men were of no interest to him. Amon, Matthias and Ulstra told Hanan they would be praying for him as they departed. Hanan now stood alone with Markus, but instead of showing concern for himself, he asked, "What have you done with the man called Jesus?"

Hanan's question took Markus by surprise, and he hesitated. "Why are you concerned about the man called Jesus? Surely he was not a part of your thievery."

"No! Jesus is the Son of God, and I must see Him. I want to have His blessing, just as He blessed my mother."

Markus realized he had not asked the name of the man he was going to take to jail. "What is your name?"

"My name is Hanan. I'm the son of Nathan, whom you murdered because he resisted you taking all of his cattle."

"Hanan, I did not murder your father, nor did I take anything from him."

"It might not have been you personally, but it was the Roman rulers who caused my mother and me to struggle just for food."

"So you thought that gave you a right to steal from those who rule over you?"

"I felt that way, yet I know I was wrong."

"Well, Hanan, I must take you into custody. You have caused my fellow soldiers to be put to death. I must say you were very good in your craft, but it has probably cost you your life."

"Would you take me to see Jesus?"

"The man called Jesus is in jail and no one may see Him. I have only been assigned to find you and now that I have, I look forward to separating myself from you, your accomplice Shiam, and Jesus."

Hanan walked alongside Markus as he was led to jail. He hoped he would not be in the same cell with Shiam, but he earnestly hoped he could see Jesus.

CHAPTER THIRTY-FIVE

Barabbas was no ordinary thief. He had a strong following of admirers. He laughed at the Roman soldiers and flaunted his ability to outsmart them. But Barabbas had been taken into custody, for the rulers could not tolerate his taunting and stealing anymore. As Barabbas was led into the jail, he heard the lashing of a whip and he flinched each time he heard it snap. Just before he was thrown into his cell, two Roman guards passed by, dragging a man who obviously had been the one receiving the lashes of the whip. The man's back was bloody. He had to be held up by His shoulders as they dragged Him down the hall. Barabbas felt a chill as his eyes looked into the beaten man's eyes. He knew instantly who the man was—he had looked into those eyes before, when he saw the man cast the money changers from the temple. It was the man called Jesus.

Barabbas saw he had a cellmate. He started to ask the man his name, but then he realized he knew the man. "Shiam, I see they have caught onto your game of stealing from the Empire. Why are you cowering in the corner? Come out and talk with me."

Shiam slowly got up and walked towards Barabbas. "Barabbas, did you hear the soldiers beating the man called Jesus?"

"I heard them, and I saw them bring Jesus down the hall. They had ripped his back to where it was bleeding very badly. I have seen Him before." Barabbas laughed. "He had a multitude of followers, until they found out He was not going to be their king and destroy the Roman Empire. I, Barabbas, have more people following me than this Jesus. Listen to the mob in the streets. They are shouting for me. No one is shouting for Jesus to be released." Barabbas laughed again and said, "Maybe they will make me king."

The timid, weak Shiam looked at Barabbas with disgust, but at the same time admired his assuredness. He asked Barabbas, "What do you think they will do with us?"

Barabbas laughed and replied, "Who knows. John the Baptist lost his head, but he was a religious leader. Jesus is a religious leader, so He perhaps will face the same fate. Even I could lose my head, for I have stirred the people up and they follow me. You, on the other hand, Shiam, could be released for you do not have anyone following you at all."

Barabbas laughed loudly as he looked at the small man in front of him. "Yes, Shiam, you they may have mercy on, but I will not beg for their mercy. I will face whatever comes."

CHAPTER THIRTY-SIX

Markus had respect for Hanan: although he was a thief, he was also a man of character, who committed himself to caring for his mother. Hanan had told him the complete story of his life and confessed to stealing the governor's necklace. Hanan's strong desire to see Jesus caused Markus to want to talk with Jesus as well, but he was glad he had not been assigned to handle the case against the Teacher.

Markus told Hanan, "Hanan, the man you want to meet has just received lashes from a soldier's whip. He is in no condition for visitors. He has disturbed my superiors greatly and the people who believed in Him have now turned against Him. My people want to dispose of Jesus and your own people are encouraging it."

Hanan knew that Matthias, Amos, Ulstra and their community were not among those who had turned against Jesus. He thought of his mother and remembered the day she had received her blessing from God's Son. He wanted so much to see Jesus, but now he realized that he never would.

CHAPTER THIRTY-SEVEN

Darius was on guard duty at the jail. His thoughts were about Markus, who had given him a new start in life. He admired Markus and was using him as an example of a good soldier. He also thought about the man called Jesus. Darius had kept up with all the trials of Jesus, and knew that the teacher's fate, as he submitted to the beatings by the Romans, had caused many to wonder if he was truly the Son of God. Darius's superiors wanted to free the man whose own people had now turned against Him.

Darius had heard murmurings among the guards about how the prisoners were to be executed. They would be nailed to a cross, hung up for all to see, dying a slow, painful death. The Roman leaders believed that such a public display would dissuade would-be troublemakers from stealing from them or from inciting others to follow anyone besides the Romans.

Markus was also at the prison, talking to Janus his captain. He wasn't pleased at what he was hearing.

"Markus, I have listened to your request to be relieved from the duty of punishing the prisoners. Your request is denied. You did an honorable job of bringing in the two men who took part in robbing from us. I want you to bring it all to closure, so you will be in charge of their executions."

Markus felt his chest tighten as he pictured Hanan and Shiam being nailed to a cross. He had never really had a close encounter with Jesus but the thought of having to watch Jesus nailed to a cross bothered him even more, knowing He had not committed any offenses against the Roman government. Markus had never been involved in a crucifixion and he had always believed it to be barbaric. Now people he had been dealing with would be led by him to meet this fate. The Preacher, Healer, the One who claimed to be God's Son would be handled by someone else, and Markus was thankful for that.

It was the day that the Jewish people celebrated Passover, a once-a-year event to commemorate the remembrance of God leading them out of Egyptian bondage. It was a custom of the Roman rulers to let one prisoner be pardoned at this time each year. The Roman rulers did not care much as to who was released, but the Jewish temple leaders did. Feeling threatened by Jesus and His following, they were in a fanatical state of mind, stirring up the people to help achieve their purposes.

Markus felt the crowd's extreme emotions and their mob-like attitudes sent a chill up his spine. He wondered, *Will I have to lead soldiers against these frantic people?* Jesus stood before Pilate, and although He was a beaten, bruised man, He had a radiance about Him that separated Him from all those around. Jesus had been whipped and a crown of jagged thorns placed on His head for a crown.

Pilate had tried to wash his hands of the responsibility of Jesus, but it had been placed back upon him. The crowd of people that gathered to watch the proceedings was large, but there was a chilling silence as everyone waited for Pilate to decide the fate of the man called Jesus.

Pilate considered the threat that each prisoner posed to the Empire. He had no issue with the thieves Hanan and Shiam, and Barabbas had been a thorn in his side long enough. Barabbas had been an arrogant, trouble-making thief—he did have a following, but Pilate thought he could control them.

On the other hand, this man called Jesus was a troublemaker of another sorts. He too had a following, but many had stopped following Him because He would not proclaim Himself king. He had stolen nothing—in fact He had said on one occasion, "Render unto Caesar what is Caesar's, and unto God what is God's." At the same time, Jesus caused him alarm—not for any aggressive action but instead for His gentle power of persuasiveness—and Pilate did not want to be responsible for His death.

Jesus had not offered any resistance to His capture, telling His followers He was giving Himself as an offering that would cleanse the sins of all who would believe in Him. It was a peacemaking sacrifice, but the crowd showed no signs of being peaceful. It was as if they were in an arena watching a deadly sporting event. Normally, Pilate was sure and certain and did not show any signs of weakness, but Jesus had caused his heart to fear, and the fear showed on his face and in his actions. He thought he had a plan that would absolve him of responsibility.

Pilate wasn't sure which way the crowd would go in making their decision, but he knew he must act.

"I have the authority to release one prisoner, as is the custom. Whom shall I release? Barabbas or the man called Jesus?"

Markus could not believe what he was hearing when the crowd began to shout. "Barabbas! Barabbas! Release Barabbas!"

Pilate held up his hand to quiet the mob of people. "What then shall I do with the man called Jesus?"

Once again, Markus heard the out-of-control mob chant, "Crucify Him! Crucify Him! Crucify Him!"

Markus felt himself tremble as Pilate held up his hand, commanding silence. Jesus was led away. Markus had heard Jesus admit to being the Son of God. Markus's thoughts took him back to the time Pilate was questioning Jesus. Pilate had asked, "Don't you know I have the power to free or crucify you?"

Markus remembered Jesus calmly but boldly answered, "You would have no power over me if it were not given to you from above."

Markus wondered if Pilate would punish Jesus harshly for such an answer, but Pilate seemed to be drugged by the spirit of the man who would admit to being the Son of God. Jesus was exuding this same spirit as he stood before Pilate for sentencing, causing Markus to ponder if this man may be who He says He is. Markus was having difficulty breathing as his chest tightened. He would do his duty, but with fear and trembling as never before.

"Guard," said Pilate, looking directly at Markus, "take this man to be crucified."

Markus realized that now Jesus would be among the prisoners he was in charge of. It troubled him concerning Shiam and Hanan, but nailing Jesus to the cross would take the muster of all of his training as a soldier.

Markus had assigned the task of leading Hanan and Shiam up Golgotha, the skull-shaped hill just outside the gates of Jerusalem where the execution would take place, to another group of soldiers. He decided the best way to overcome his anxiety concerning the man called Jesus was to lead Him there himself.

Crucifixion was a cruel way to take someone's life, and this time it troubled Markus deeply. He looked at Jesus carrying His cross, and saw the man was so badly beaten and bruised that getting the cross to the top of the hill would be difficult.

The throng stirred with emotion as Markus had never seen before. There were people jeering and spitting at Jesus. There were a few people weeping and reaching out to Jesus—not in a way they could help Him, but rather that He in such agony would still help them. They seemed to just want to touch Jesus, but the soldiers kept them back. *Where are His disciples?* Markus wondered. *Where are the miracles? If this Jesus is really the Son of God, what father would watch this and not intervene?*

Markus watched as the weakened Jesus fell under the heavy load of the cross. He ordered another man to pick it up and take it up the hill. Even with the burden of the cross removed, Jesus stumbled on the stony path. His physical endurance had been tested by the extreme cruelty of the Roman soldiers. When the procession reached the top of the hill, other soldiers were getting ready to nail Hanan and Shiam to their crosses.

Shiam shook his fist at Hanan and yelled, "You caused this to happen! You and your foolish greed are causing me to lose my life! You deserve to die! I have not done anything to deserve this!"

Shiam was frantically resisting being laid on the cross, but he was no match against the burly Roman guards. The soldier drove the nails through Shiam's hands and feet.

The screams of Shiam sent a chill up Markus's spine. Shiam was still screaming as the cross was raised.

Hanan lay flat on his back across the cross. He was weeping and tears ran down his face. Bound to the rough, splintered wood, Hanan turned his head and saw Jesus the merciful Teacher with a mocking crown of thorns, blood caked on His body and pain in His eyes. Jesus was offering no resistance and it seemed to mesmerize the soldiers standing there with the hammer and the rusty nails. Markus merely nodded his head for the soldiers to go to Hanan's cross next.

Hanan was not weeping for himself, but rather for the man called Jesus, knowing that the same rough splinters that were piercing his skin were also piercing the Holy Man who had blessed his mother. He had watched as the battered Jesus walked unsteadily up the hill, as people spat at Jesus and called Him names. Hanan wished for another miracle from this man of God, one that would show all of the people that He was the promised deliverer. Hanan wanted Jesus to stand up and proclaim His heavenly power, and he did not want Jesus to suffer anymore.

Hanan longed to crawl on the ground and just touch the hem of His garment, but he felt the first nail being driven into his hand. He wanted to scream, just as Shiam had screamed, but the pain caused him to lose his breath and choke. He lay there as the soldiers drove the other two spikes into his body—one in his hand, the other into his feet. Somehow, the pain was so intense it cut off Hanan's ability to cry out. Instead he cried out inside his head, wishing for it all to end.

Hanging from the cross, Hanan, although in intense pain, watched as the soldiers drove the nails into the hands and feet of the man called Jesus. He watched as they raised Jesus up between two thieves.

Hanan could breathe only if he raised his upper body, but that increased the pain in his hands and feet. His throat was parched and his vision was blurred. He wished for life to end quickly, but the agony was drawn out, giving no clue as to when the end would come. He turned his head to see Jesus and heard Him speak: "Water, I thirst."

But the soldiers, laughing, gave him a bitter mixture to drink.

"Behold thy mother; behold thy son."

Hanan glanced down and saw the mother of Jesus. He thought of his own mother and, weeping, he inwardly asked her to forgive him.

"Father, forgive them, for they know not what they do," said the Teacher from His cross.

Then Hanan heard Shiam say with an angry voice, "If you're

God's Son, save yourself and us as well." His voice was full of ridicule, dripping with disbelief at who Jesus claimed to be.

Hanan swallowed hard and wondered if he could utter any sound. It felt like he had been hanging on the cross in pain for hours, and he realized Jesus was suffering the same excruciating pain. Shiam was bitter and Hanan was sorry he had been the cause of his suffering. Unlike Shiam, though, Hanan believed that Jesus could call for a power from God and stop it all—but Hanan realized that He was not going to, that it was not part of his holy plan.

How much time has passed since Shiam's remarks? Hanan wondered, *Did I pass out? How much longer can I stand this excruciating pain? The faces in the crowd are blurred. I can hear weeping, but I can also hear the ridiculing voices of an angry mob. The soldiers are laughing and their swords are clanging out harshly as they glance against the stones. The sun was hot and the wind was still when this all began, but now I feel the wind. It even rocks my cross. It's growing dark and I am so weak.*

As the sky darkened and the wind continued to build, Hanan through his blurred vision thought he saw Matthias. His mind was hallucinating as he saw his mother and father standing by a doorway. They were smiling and welcoming him home.

His throat was parched and he wondered if he could answer Shiam's last remark, disparaging the Teacher he so admired.

He was closer now to the man called Jesus than he had ever been, and he opened his mouth and forced out these words: "This man has done no wrong. We deserve what is happening to us. Master, when You come into Your kingdom, remember me."

Hanan could not talk anymore.

"This day thou shalt be with me in paradise."

Then Hanan heard once more the voice of the One who had blessed him.

"It is finished."

The sky grew dark and the thunder rolled. Markus looked at his soldiers gambling for Jesus's robe. He felt disgust, but more than that, as he looked upon Hanan, whom he had developed respect for, and Shiam, whom he come to know and feel sorry for, it caused his heart to ache.

Markus had purposefully kept his eyes off of the man called Jesus, but he looked up and saw a body drenched with blood, and bruised from the beatings He had endured. The body of the man called Jesus was hanging on the cross, but the spirit of the miracle worker was gone.

As the thunder continued to roll, the sky grew darker, and the wind blew violently! The ground began to shake and people lost their footing as rocks started to crack apart.

Markus felt like falling on his sword. Instead, he fell on his knees powerless in facing the forces upon him. He could only weep and cry out, "Surely this man was the Son of God!"

ABOUT THE AUTHOR

Although this is Tom Lloyd's first book, he has written stories, an array of poems, and many gospel songs. Governor Jimmie Davis of Louisiana recorded three of his songs, including "She Touched the Hem of His Garment," "Heavens Avenue," and "Soul Train to Glory."

The Man Called Jesus was inspired by Tom's daughter's encounter with the scripture concerning the thief on the cross who turned to Jesus for help.

Tom graduated from Hermitage High School in 1952, and then served two years in the United States Army. He worked for thirty-six years in the paint coatings industry. He was with Glidden Paint Company for twenty-eight years and with Devoe Paint Company for eight years.

Tom's wife Louise retired from her job with the International Mission Board as assistant facilities manager, and they now live with their daughter and her family in Chester, Virginia.

CPSIA information can be obtained
at www.ICGtesting.com
Printed in the USA
FFOW02n0342210417
34696FF